"Damn it."

His growl whispered into her mouth as he tore his lips from hers.

Stunned, her lips stinging from the pressure he'd applied, yet aching for more, Kit stared at him blankly as he strode to the door.

"I should apologize." Logan paused with his hand on the doorknob. His eyes were shuttered, refusing her a glimpse of his thoughts. His lips curved cynically. "But I won't." Turning the knob with controlled violence, he swung the door open. "Welcome home Kit," he drawled tauntingly, stepping out of the room and shutting the door with a definite snap.

Kit closed her eyes as the first tear trickled down her hot face.

Logan McKittrick had always been her champion. Why was he now behaving like an enemy?

Dear Reader,

Welcome to Silhouette! Our goal is to give you hours of unbeatable reading pleasure, and we hope you'll enjoy each month's six new Silhouette Desires. These sensual, provocative love stories are both believable and compelling—sometimes they're poignant, sometimes humorous, but always enjoyable.

Indulge yourself. Experience all the passion and excitement of falling in love along with our heroine as she meets the irresistible man of her dreams and together they overcome all obstacles in the path to a happy ending.

If this is your first Desire, I hope it'll be the first of many. If you're already a Silhouette Desire reader, thanks for your support! Look for some of your favorite authors in the coming months: Stephanie James, Diana Palmer, Dixie Browning, Ann Major and Doreen Owens Malek, to name just a few.

Happy reading!

Isabel Swift
Senior Editor

SDRL-7/85

JOAN HOHL
Nevada Silver

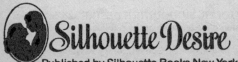

Silhouette Desire

Published by Silhouette Books New York

America's Publisher of Contemporary Romance

SILHOUETTE BOOKS
300 East 42nd St., New York, N.Y. 10017

ISBN: 0-373-05330-4

First Silhouette Books printing January 1987

America's Publisher of Contemporary Romance

Printed in the U.S.A.

Books by Joan Hohl

Silhouette Special Edition

Thorne's Way #54

Silhouette Intimate Moments

Moments Harsh, Moments Gentle #35

Silhouette Romance

A Taste for Rich Things #334
Someone Waiting #358
The Scent of Lilacs #376

Silhouette Desire

A Much Needed Holiday #247
*Texas Gold #294
*California Copper #312
*Nevada Silver #330

**Desire Trilogy

JOAN HOHL,

a Gemini and an inveterate daydreamer, says she always has her head in the clouds. Though she reads eight or nine books a week, she only discovered romances ten years ago. "But as soon as I read one," she confesses, "I was hooked." Now an extremely popular author, she is thrilled to be getting paid for exactly what she loves doing best. Joan Hohl also writes under the pseudonym Amii Lorin.

For my agent, Evan Marshall...a friend indeed!

One

"So, you finally decided to come home, did you?"

Stepping into the room, Kit Aimsley shut the door quietly and leaned back against it.

"This is *not* my home, this is my office," she responded, somewhat amazed at the steadiness of her tone. "And what are you doing in it?" Her expressionless face and coolly arched, pale eyebrows revealed nothing of the emotions leaping crazily inside her mind and body as she stared at the man she loved.

"Takin' care of business." Logan McKittrick smiled wryly. "It's a rotten job—but somebody has to do it."

Moving into the room, Kit ran a hungry gaze over his impressive form from beneath lowered lashes. Lord, he looked good, too good! Today there was very little evidence of the earthy rancher about Logan's appearance. Attired in an expensive-looking, obviously hand-tailored three-piece business suit, Logan had more the look of the boardroom than broad spaces. The rich brown shade of the suit brought out the red in his auburn hair; the pristine white of his shirt contrasted with the deep tan of his skin; the swirled gold, brown and white of his patterned tie hinted at the debonair side of his character.

In total, Logan McKittrick presented an attractive picture of sheer masculine individuality.

Kit Aimsley had loved Logan all her life; she had been *in* love with him for over eight years, ever since her seventeenth summer.

"Don't be cute, Logan, it's simply not you." Flipping her long, silvery blond hair back with one hand, Kit perched on the end of the desk and stared challengingly into his cool green eyes.

"You've been gone for over two weeks." Ignoring her chiding remark, Logan stated the obvious.

"That's right." Kit smiled mockingly. "And I'll be going back to the coast in a couple months." From behind her facade of composure, she waited for his reaction . . . it was swift in coming.

Heaving his long frame off the desk chair, Logan towered over her, his emerald eyes glinting with anger. "Damn it, Kathryn, what keeps you running back to California?" he demanded in a shiver-causing, too soft tone.

Oh, yes, he's angry, Kit decided, stiffening her spine. Not only had he called her by her given name, Kathryn, which he only did when he was very annoyed with her, but his tone had dropped to the level she privately thought of as flash-point soft. Keeping her own tone even was not the easiest thing Kit had ever done; facing him calmly was even more difficult.

"California's my home." Watching his eyes narrow, Kit slid off the edge of the desk with apparent nonchalance, striving to appear disinterested with the subject, while putting distance between them.

"Bull."

Oh, dear. Kit sauntered to the other side of the suddenly too small office. Logan became crude only when he was spoiling for a fight. As she moved away from him, she arched her pale brows disdainfully.

"I beg your pardon?" Her last word came out jagged. All the moisture dried in her throat as Logan slowly circled around the desk.

"You heard me." Logan's tone dropped another octave. "Nevada is as much home to you as California." His loose-limbed gait quickly closed the distance between them. "While you were growing up you spent as much time here as you did in California."

Denial was impossible for Kit; Logan's claim was true. She backed up again, then halted abruptly as her spine made contact with the wall. "But—" Kit had to pause to wet her dry lips "—my family's in California."

A spasm of emotion washed over Logan's harshly chiseled features, then was controlled before Kit could identify the expression. His lips thinned into a straight, uncompromising line.

"And I'm not family?" Logan came to a stop a foot from her; his glittering gaze pinned her to the wall.

"Yes, of course you are." Though Kit was quick to respond, despair chilled her. Logan's question encapsulated her dilemma—she loved him as a man; he loved her as a young, indulged sister. Refusing to acknowledge the sting of tears in her eyes, Kit gazed at him directly. "And that's why I'm supposed to bring you back to California with me when I go."

Logan's eyes widened a fraction. "What's why you're suppose to bring me back with you?" he snapped.

"For Zack's wedding," Kit explained hurriedly, recognizing the signs of Logan's dwindling patience. But, if nothing else, her statement about her brother Zack's plans to marry brought a spark of amusement to Logan's eyes.

"Caught up with her, did he?" Logan mused softly.

Kit frowned. What was that remark supposed to mean? "Her? What do you know about Aubrey?" Kit demanded suspiciously.

"Not much," Logan admitted. "I saw her performance here in Tahoe a couple weeks ago. Onstage, she's dynamite."

"I wouldn't know," Kit muttered, hating the twinge of jealously that unfurled inside. She genuinely liked the lovely woman her brother had chosen to spend his life with. Kit felt demeaned by the feeling of envy. Damn, she groaned inwardly, why couldn't she feel about Logan the same as she felt about her twin half brothers, Zack and Thack? Why had Logan kissed her that summer she graduated from high school? Why was she tormenting herself with unanswerable questions?

Muffling a sigh, Kit edged around him to walk to the chair placed at the corner of the desk. "Was that when you spoke with Zack?" she probed, sinking onto

the leather seat. "When you caught Aubrey's performance?" she clarified.

"Yes." Logan stalked her like a shadow. Skirting
the chair, he sat on the edge of the desk.

Kit's gaze noted the way the material of his slacks
tautened over the long, hard muscles of the thigh that
rested on the desk. Feeling a tightness in her throat,
she glanced away. Why, oh, why must she suffer this
attraction to him? Another unanswerable query.

"Zack gave you my message?"

Kit's gaze sliced back to his gleaming eyes. "Ver-
batim, I think," she replied dryly. "Wasn't it, 'Tell the
brat I want to talk to her'?" Kit managed a haughty
expression.

Logan laughed. Kit's insides turned to water at the
rich sound of his amusement. Still chuckling, he
cocked a dark brow at her. "So, why didn't you call?"

Kit was suddenly angry. Angry and frustrated.
"Call? Why should I?" she asked, glaring at him. "I
had been calling you for weeks before leaving for California!" Her lips curled. "Your ranch foreman informed me that you were much too busy to be
bothered." Kit clamped her lips together to contain the
spate of indignant fury she longed to fling at him.

"And that twisted your pretty little nose out of
joint, hmm?" Leaning to her, Logan tweaked her
nose.

"Logan..." Kit began warningly, only to gasp for
breath as his fingers brushed her cheek then cupped
her chin. As he tilted her face up, he lowered his head.
Kit's senses swam from the impact of his nearness, and
his earthy, spicy scent.

"I *was* busy, you brat," he murmured, eliciting a shudder from her by gliding the tip of a finger over her lips. "We have you spoiled, Zack and I." Logan's lips quirked in a cynical smile. "It's time you learned that we can't drop whatever we're doing at the snap of your fingers."

Stung, Kit jerked her head back, away from his touch, and banged her head against the back of the seat with her impetuous action. Logan's smile infuriated her.

"I have never expected either Zack or you to dance attendance on me!" Kit protested, rubbing the back of her head and ruffling the smoothness of her silvery-sheened hair. "You...you both treat me like a child!" she sputtered. "I am twenty-five years old, Logan!"

"And I was already a teenager when you were born," Logan retorted, reaching around her to probe the sore spot on her head with rough, yet amazingly gentle fingers. "Thirteen to be exact, and Zack was ten." His fingers continued to stroke Kit's now tingling scalp as he went on, musingly, "I suppose it was only natural for Zack and me to coddle you—you were such a pretty little thing, all big blue eyes and shiny white hair."

"But I'm not a *little* thing any longer, Logan," Kit pointed out in a breathy whisper, praying he'd remove his hand from her head, hoping he wouldn't.

"That's true." Logan smiled derisively, then continued to probe, asking Kit about Thackery, the Sharp brother who had just been reunited with his family. "Is Thackery going to be yet another slave at your narrow, elegant feet?"

Narrow, elegant feet! Kit had to squelch an urge to glance down. Did Logan really think . . . She caught herself up short. Damn him! Now not only was her scalp tingling, but her toes were as well! Drawing a steadying breath, Kit shook his hand away with a sharp move of her head. Logan's soft laughter caused a shocking spear of pain in her chest.

"I doubt it," she snapped, furious at him. "At the moment, Thack is thoroughly occupied with being a slave at his bride's feet."

"Thack?" Logan's laughter deepened. "Zack and Thack, is it? I love it." He shook his head, dislodging the neatly brushed auburn mane. The tingle spread to Kit's fingers. Suddenly she itched with the need to smooth back the thick strands of hair glinting with red highlights. Logan drew a silent sigh from her by brushing his hair back impatiently.

"So, what is Thack like?" His teasing tone had given way to genuine interest. Straightening, he swung his leg easily. The ripple of muscle beneath the fine material of his slacks sent a shaft of heat through Kit's body. She forced herself to concentrate on his question out of sheer desperation.

"Like Zack, only different," she answered vaguely.

Logan raised his green eyes as if beseeching help from above. "Could you possibly be a tad more specific, Kit?" he taunted.

Well, at least she was Kit again, she acknowledged gratefully. Apparently Logan's anger had subsided. Kit shivered delicately. Angry, Logan both frightened and excited her in a way she didn't fully understand— or want to.

"I don't know quite how to explain it." Kit shrugged helplessly. "They're very similar in looks as well as in character. When I ran into Zack's place and saw Thack standing at the window, I honestly thought it was Zack. They are that identical." Kit shook her head as if to clear it. "But, on closer inspection, they are different." Her shoulders lifted, then fell. "I can't explain it. You'll have to see for yourself."

"When we go to the coast for Zack's wedding," Logan inserted smoothly.

"Yes," Kit agreed shakily, feeling herself grow weak over his use of the term *we*.

"And Thack's newly married?" Logan persisted with his interrogation.

"Yes," Kit repeated, not at all resentful of his interest. As the admired and loved stepson of Kit's father, Logan had always been accepted as a member of the family. Logan was...Logan. Kit couldn't remember a time when she hadn't adored him.

"And?" Logan asked, reminding her that he was waiting. "Did you like her?"

"Oh!" Kit blinked. "Very much. Her name's Barbara. She's obviously crazy about Thack." Kit smiled. "She's tall and slender." Her gaze skimmed over his hair, then settled on his eyes. "You know," she mused. "Barbara's hair and eyes are quite like yours, except her eyes are more hazel than green." A soft sigh whispered through her lips. "She's beautiful."

She's beautiful. Logan felt his stomach clench. Narrowing his eyes, he studied Kit through dark, blunt lashes, drinking in the sight of her like a man dying of thirst. As far as Logan was concerned, Kit was the most beautiful creature on God's green earth. A vision of her had tormented him every second of the time she'd been in California, as the reality of her did when she was in Nevada.

Above average in height, Kit's chin was on a level with Logan's lips when she stood before him. Though slender, her form was curved and rounded softly, her breasts full and high. Her eyes were ever-changing blue, at times clear as a summer sky, at others deep as a mountain lake. Her nose was small and delicately fashioned, her cheeks curved gently. And her mouth! Logan groaned silently. Kit's mouth was the source of every one of his erotic dreams.

Kathryn. Kit. Brat.

Damn.

His stomach twisted another notch. Logan had gritted his teeth when she'd bumped her head . . . a reflexive, ingrained action camouflaging the alarm he felt. When Kit felt pain, Logan felt pain. It had been thus ever since his first glimpse of her at the advanced age of two weeks. At thirteen, Logan had happily taken on the role of big brother. Protecting Kit was not a chore; it was a way of life. Loving Kit was unquestioned.

His expression unknowingly brooding, Logan stared bleakly into the adored face of his young stepsister—who no longer was.

Hard, sexual awareness made Logan feel both intensely excited and depressingly sick. He was almost used to the inner conflict. He'd lived with it for over eight years.

Why, why, why had he given in to that sudden, overwhelming desire to kiss Kit the evening of her high school graduation party? Logan was all too aware of the answer to his question. He had kissed her, really kissed her, because he could no longer resist the need to do so.

The need to taste Kit had started burning in Logan sometime between Kit's sixteenth and seventeenth birthdays. It was at that time, consumed with self-loathing, that Logan had begun retreating from Kit's family to northern Nevada, where the ranch his natural father had left to him was located.

Now, gazing into Kit's eyes, Logan fought against the recurring urge to taste, caress, possess Kathryn Aimsley, his self-adopted sister. Self-disgust was an accepted constant. Kit regarded him in the same way she did Zack, and very likely, now Thack. Kit trusted Logan McKittrick. Logan McKittrick ached to betray that trust.

"Logan?" Kit was growing decidedly uncomfortable with each passing second of his slit-eyed regard. Was Logan's anger building again? Kit sighed. With each of her birthdays, Logan grew more remote and less patient with her.

"What?" Distraction rather than impatience could be heard in Logan's tone. "What was the question?" He frowned.

"You—" Kit wet her lips "—you seemed so far away. Is something wrong?"

"No." Logan exhaled, deeply, slowly. "I've got things on my mind." Once again his lips curved cynically. "Has Zack set a definite date for the wedding?" Logan deliberately led the subject away from himself.

"Not yet." Though Kit eyed him speculatively, she went along with his topic change. "He told me he'd call us as soon as the date's been set."

Logan nodded. "Good enough." He slid off the desk abruptly and began to prowl around the small room. Watching him warily, Kit bit back a gasp when he swung toward her. "Are you planning to stay put here awhile?" His lips twisted. "Or did you meet some terribly interesting young member of the legendary 'fast lane' during your visit to the coast?"

Rattled and confused, Kit gaped at him in bewilderment for long moments. Then a slow anger began burning inside. This was not the first time Logan had presumed to refer to some *man* in her life. And, usually, his reference was made in a sarcastic or accusatory manner.

Meeting his glittering stare defiantly, Kit fanned her simmering anger into a blaze. Logan was beginning to carry his big brother routine just a bit too far. Hadn't she just reminded him that she was no longer a child?

"Yes, I plan to stay," Kit lashed out at him hotly. "We have a sale pending on this damned casino—remember?"

"This *damned* casino is earning you a respectable income," Logan retaliated, striding to the chair to loom over her. "And I distinctly remember telling you I have not decided if I want to sell my interest in it." Bracing his hands on the arms of the chair, he bent over her. "Your father left this casino to us in good faith. I feel sure selling it was not what he had in mind when he chose us as his heirs."

The gritty sound of his voice grated on Kit's nerves; his warm breath misted her lips and created havoc with her senses. Kit found the simple act of speaking almost beyond her.

"I-I don't like it here, Logan," she muttered.

"What are you talking about?" he demanded. "You always said you loved Tahoe!"

"I do!" Kit raked the slender fingers of one hand through her hair, and bit down on her lip. "I loved visiting here with Dad. But I hate running this casino." Sighing, she let her hand fall into her lap. "Don't you understand, Logan? It's not the same anymore." Kit could have admitted that what she hated most was that *he* was rarely there anymore, but she didn't.

"Oh, I understand perfectly," Logan said, his voice very soft. "When you came here with your father, you were playing—" his smile sent a shaft of pain straight through Kit's heart "—the California socialite on a gambling spree," he gibed. "But now the beautiful, indulged daughter of a wealthy entrepreneur has discovered that one occasionally gets one's hands dirty while raking in the money and she hates it."

"That's not fair, Logan." Kit was close to tears, but determined she'd shed none in front of him. "You know I'm not afraid of hard work or getting my hands dirty. I've done both, countless times at your ranch."

Irrefutable truth, and Logan *did* know it. Sheer male jealously kept him jabbing at her and wounding himself.

"Then it must be a man." Logan's mouth was almost touching hers, and it was killing him. "A new one, Kit? Some pretty California swinger?"

Kit's lips trembled, not from fear but with hunger. Logan's mouth was so close to hers, so close. If she moved just a fraction, she'd bring their lips into contact. Aching to relive the feel of his mouth devouring hers, yet afraid of his reaction and rejection, Kit forced herself to remain very still.

"There have always been hordes of males around you." Logan's voice had dropped to a harsh whisper. "Have you finally decided to settle on one?" He put into words the fear that had been eating at his mind and insides ever since she'd failed to return to Tahoe after a week's visit with her brothers.

"That is none of your damned business," Kit hissed, sitting rigidly, as if frozen. "I would refuse to answer a question put to me like that from either Zack or Thack. I certainly won't respond to it from *you*." Kit bit her lip as she uttered the insult. She felt Logan stiffen, then felt his breath as he expelled it sharply, then heard his softly growled warning.

"Watch your mouth, brat. I'm as good as a member of the family." He raised his head slightly, enough to drill her with his narrow-eyed gaze. "But, as you've so gently pointed out, I'm not blood family, am I?" Kit stopped breathing at the sight of the glow that lit his eyes. "Why shouldn't I sample what so many have tasted before me?"

Startled by his grating tone, incensed by his words, Kit opened her mouth to protest. With the quickness of a bird of prey, Logan's head swooped down. His mouth fastened on to her parted lips.

Logan's kiss was very brief and thoroughly demoralizing.

"Damn it." His growl whispered into her mouth as he tore his lips from hers.

Stunned, her lips stinging from the pressure he'd applied, yet aching for more, Kit stared at him blankly as he strode to the door.

"I should apologize." Logan paused with his hand on the doorknob. His eyes were shuttered, refusing her a glimpse of his thoughts. His lips curved cynically. "But I won't." Turning the knob with controlled violence, he swung the door open. "Welcome home, Kit," he drawled, stepping out of the room and shutting the door with a definite snap.

Shaken, Kit sat absolutely still for long moments, her gaze lingering on the door. What had happened? What had she done to warrant the disdain Logan had meted out to her?

Kit closed her eyes as the first tear trickled down her hot face.

Logan McKittrick had always been her champion. Why was he now behaving like an enemy?

Impatiently brushing the stream of tears from her cheeks, Kit stood and walked unsteadily to her chair behind the desk. Slumped into the supple leather, she imagined she could feel the warmth of Logan's body.

How long had Logan been in *her* chair, behind *her* desk? Kit wondered, her fingers toying with a gold-toned pen lying on the desk's scarred surface. On his return to California from Tahoe, Zack had told her he'd talked to Logan. That had been five days after she'd left Nevada for the coast.

Had Logan commandeered her office mere days after she'd left it? Kit frowned. She'd been begging him to come to the casino in Tahoe for weeks before leaving for Zack's place on the California coast. Logan hadn't even deigned to speak to her on the phone.

His foreman, a friend of Kit's since she was small, had claimed Logan was too busy with ranch business to talk to her.

But then, if Logan was so busy with the ranch, why had he suddenly arrived at the casino? Had he known she'd left?

Deciding that speculation was getting her nowhere, Kit buzzed her manager's office, requesting his presence in her office at once.

"Hi, Kit. I didn't know you were back." Mike Harmon grinned a welcome as he sauntered into her office. "You wanted to see me?"

"Yes." Kit smiled. Having utilized the time required for Mike's secretary to locate him on the casino floor to repair her tear-streaked makeup, her composure was intact. "Sit down, Mike." Kit gestured at the chair at the corner of the desk.

Kit ran an assessing glance over her casino manager as he moved to comply. Mike stood approximately six feet tall, even in height with Logan. There the similarity between the two men ended. Mike was elegantly slim in comparison to Logan's rangy muscularity. His features were finely sculpted, whereas Logan's were harshly etched. Attired impeccably, Mike projected an image reminiscent of a Regency dandy, an image that was the opposite of Logan's rawboned frontiersman aura.

"Did you have a pleasant vacation, Kit?" Mike's naturally low, culturally trained voice was like a balm to Kit's frayed nerves.

All the strain went out of Kit's smile. "I had a very pleasant vacation, thank you." Leaning forward, she rested her arms on the desk. "And how did things go here?'' Kit probed, in hopes of finding out the length of Logan's tenure at her desk.

Mike's shrug was eloquent. ''As usual. The Silver Lining runs on well-greased wheels.'' He reinforced his assurance with an easy smile.

The Silver Lining was the name Kit's father, Bruce Aimsley, had dubbed the casino on purchasing it twenty years before. His whim had paid off handsomely, as it had certainly lined his pockets with an abundance of silver. Now it was continuing to line Kit's and, to a lesser degree, Logan's pockets.

''You've had no problems at all?'' Kit sank her probe a little deeper.

''Nothing to speak of.'' Relaxing in front of Kit, as he rarely did in front of anybody, Mike stretched out his long legs, crossing his silk-hose clad ankles. Tilting his head, he gazed at her with mild curiosity. ''You had reason to suspect that there had been problems?''

''Only the fact that I found Logan McKittrick at my desk when I returned,'' Kit replied bluntly.

''Ah, yes, big brother Logan.'' Mike's trace of a smile hinted at a wealth of inner amusement. ''Let's just say that Logan helped grease the casino wheels.''

Suspicious of his smile, Kit came to attention. ''Did Logan give you any flak?'' she demanded.

''Flak?'' Mike now laughed aloud. ''Hell, no!'' His laugh subsided to a chuckle. ''Logan and I understand each other. He's arrogant. I'm careful. Together, we can handle a lot more than this little ole casino.''

Beginning to feel surrounded and out-maneuvered, Kit stared impassively at Mike. "Are you implying that I'm redundant here?" she asked softly.

"On the contrary," Mike disagreed, his amusement gleaming from his deceptively gentle blue eyes. "In my humble opinion, you are sorely needed here in Nevada."

"I'm extremely relieved to hear it," Kit drawled in a credible imitation of Logan. "Thank you for your time, Mike. I won't keep you any longer."

It wasn't until after Mike had sauntered out of her office, lips twitching with amusement, that Kit realized he'd said she was needed in Nevada, but not at the casino.

Two

Why the hell did I kiss her?

Driving back to the apartment he maintained in Tahoe, Logan lectured himself on the pitfalls of stupidity.

By now, Kit has more than likely decided you are some kind of pervert, his conscience nagged relentlessly. And, since she thinks of you as a brother, she's probably in a state of shock.

Parking the big estate wagon, Logan loped along to the elevator. Riding the lift to the fifth floor, he betrayed the agitation that hummed along his nervous system by jingling the key ring he held in his broad hand.

Should I call her? he mused, the keys rattling in his palm as he strode to the door of his apartment. He could plead the excuse of tiredness, or tension, or temporary insanity.

Temporary insanity! A derisive smile twisted his lips as he entered the flat and tossed the keys onto the nearest table. There wasn't a damn thing temporary about the type of insanity riding his mind and body.

Love, buddy, that's the name of your particular brand of madness, not infatuation or even old-fashioned, garden-variety physical attraction, Logan mocked himself, moving toward the wet bar that took up most of one wall.

Splashing aged whiskey into a squat glass, Logan took a long swallow of his drink, then strolled to the velour pit couch in the austerely decorated room. Sprawling on the curved couch, he stared morosely into the amber liquid.

Logan loves Kathryn, he recited to himself wryly.

Damn! Why does Logan love Kathryn? Logan smiled—wryly. That one was easy enough to answer.

Kathryn Aimsley was beautiful, outgoing, fun to be with, and sexy as hell.

She was also intelligent, honest, a true friend, and sexy as hell.

In addition, she had proved herself a hard worker, a savvy businesswoman, and sexy as hell.

Logan dumped the rest of his drink down his suddenly parched throat. Kathryn was sexy, and Logan was hurting—in all kinds of places.

Pushing his long body from the couch, Logan ambled back to the bar. He was tipping the bottle over his empty glass when an errant thought struck: *Why shouldn't Logan love Kathryn?*

Frowning, he made his way back to the couch, completely forgetting the drink he'd been about to pour for himself. Shrugging out of his jacket and vest, he sat on the edge of the couch to tug the seldom-worn, hand-made Italian shoes from his feet. Exhaling deeply, he carefully stretched his body around the curving couch and stared at the eggshell-toned wall opposite.

Why shouldn't Logan love Kathryn?

Eyelids narrowing over green eyes gleaming with thought, Logan marshaled reasons for and against a relationship with Kit.

Granted, Kit had always been like a sister to him—but she really wasn't his sister. So, there was no reason prohibiting a relationship. And, even though Kit looked on him as she did her other brothers, Logan knew he was capable of quickly changing that notion—oh was he capable!

Then, of course, there was the difference in their ages. But an age gap that had seemed a chasm when she was seventeen and he was thirty didn't appear quite so wide now that Kit was twenty-five and Logan was thirty-eight.

The bottom line, Logan realized, was that Kit was a woman, fully capable of making an adult decision, whereas eight years previously she'd been a young, impressionable girl, reacting to the stimuli of the moment.

One particular moment sprang to mind, and Logan shivered with the memory. Talk about stimuli! Closing his eyes, he allowed his mind to replay the experience of that soft summer night in Palm Springs.

Laureen and Bruce Aimsley had thrown the large house open for a gala party in celebration of Kit's graduation from high school. Since Bruce's business interests were far flung and varied, there were all sorts of people there in addition to Kit's friends and classmates. Logan had recognized several representatives from the film industry, a few guests from the art world, and even more of the group from Lake Tahoe, Reno and Las Vegas.

The party had started early and ended very late, long after Logan had made his escape. Parties had never been Logan's favorite thing. Throughout the late afternoon and into the early perfect California evening Logan had circulated, mingling with the guests as he sampled the delicious food Laureen had specially ordered from the very best caterers, and guzzling his fair share of the excellent liquor Bruce had provided.

Later, when he was alone, Logan had attempted to assure himself that his actions were the direct result of imbibing too liberally. That reasoning hadn't worked though—his conscience merely sneered. He had known full well what he was doing every damned minute. And, in retrospect, Logan clearly remembered every minute of time he'd spent at that party.

Most of the young people, including Kit, had spent the majority of the afternoon in the pool, the boys and young men laughing, the girls shrieking. Observing the horseplay in the sparkling blue water of the Aimsleys' kidney-shaped pool, Logan had determined that should any one of the boys or men grab Kit in any one of the wrong spots on her budding anatomy, that male would be fortunate to come out of the pool with his life, let alone his beautifully capped teeth.

The young people had abandoned the pool soon after sundown, not to rest, but to dance. While chatting amiably with all and sundry, Logan had never lost sight of Kit. On noting an unbelievably handsome young man cajole her away from the crowd, he excused himself politely and, lips flattening in anger, unabashedly followed them to Bruce's dark, deserted study. The door to the room was ajar an inch or so. Pausing outside the study, he heard the young man's thickened tone.

"Ah, c'm'on, Kitten, you can do better than that," the would-be seducer complained. Logan had detested the sobriquet "Kitten" ever since.

"Maybe I can," Kit replied calmly, "but I won't. You've had the kiss I owed you, now let's go back to the party."

"One more, honey," the young man demanded more than pleaded. "And make this a juicy one."

With the silence natural to him, Logan slipped into the darkened room, green eyes glittering like a cat's on the scent of prey.

"Darren, stop." Kit's tone held a note of entreaty.

"Darren—stop." Logan's tone was threaded with steel. Having reached Bruce's desk, he switched the goose-necked desk lamp on.

After a confused blink, the young man threw out his smooth chin.

"Who the hell do you think you are?" he blustered. "And what the hell do you think you're doing?"

"Logan!" Kit's soft exclamation went unheard in the tension-filled room.

"The name's McKittrick," Logan replied pleas- antly, moving toward the young man and grasping the collar of his two-hundred-dollar shirt. "And I'm ejecting you from this room." As he spoke he marched the sputtering man to, then through, the doorway.

"I'm a guest here! You can't do this to me!" young handsome declared.

"I just did." Logan closed the door in his face.

"Logan, really!" Kit exclaimed heatedly. "What *do* you think you're doing—defending my honor?"

Turning from the door, Logan walked to her slowly. "Something like that," he murmured, sweeping her with a narrow-eyed glance that settled on her red- dened lips. "Did pretty boy hurt you in any way?" he asked with forced calm.

"No, he did not hurt me." Her burgeoning breasts heaved with her sharp exhalation, drawing his gaze, and unwanted arousal. "I can handle *him*." She dis- missed the young man with a toss of her head that sent the silver strands of her hair flaring around her slen- der shoulders.

"But, can you handle me?" Stepping to within inches of her, Logan stared into her widened eyes and asked himself what the hell he *did* think he was doing. Expecting her to laugh, dance away from him, or even punch him on the arm as she'd often done before, Logan was thrown off balance when Kit smiled in a very adult, decidedly sensuous way.

"There's only one way you'll ever find that out, isn't there?" Kit's breathy voice was loaded with sheer challenge.

Logan fought an inner battle with himself for all of thirty seconds, then he broke under the longing, frustration and intense need he'd been living with for more months than he wanted to remember. Months, moreover, in which he'd refused to assuage his hunger with another woman . . . any other woman.

Too aware of the tremor in the fingers he raised to cradle her chin, Logan lifted her face as he lowered his head. Exerting more control than he'd believed himself capable of, he brushed his lips over hers, lightly, gently. Even then he might have saved himself eight years of gnawing emptiness, had Kit not moaned softly and parted her lips willingly.

Hungrier than he'd ever been before in his life, Logan took her mouth ravenously while his arms circled her body to crush it to his. Kit's soft curves molded pliantly to his hard angles, setting his mind on hold and his body on fire.

Lying on the pit couch, eyes tightly closed, Logan shuddered as the memory set off a blast of desire in his body that sent sharp shards of need rushing through his system. Now, as then, Logan lost sight of everything but a hunger only Kit could appease.

In retrospect, Logan knew it would have been bad enough had he released Kit then, been satisfied with the warm pliancy of her lips and body. But he hadn't been satisfied, hadn't released her.

Senses overwhelming sense, Logan trailed his hand down Kit's delicate spine, around the indentation of her small waist, then up her rib cage to capture one upthrust breast in his broad hand. The stab of her aroused, tightened nipple electrified him into action.

Reason gone, his entire being centered on possessing the only woman who'd ever had the power to drive him wild with need, Logan moved unerringly to the long, leather-covered sofa that flanked the fireplace, his mouth still fused to hers.

"Logan. Logan," Kit whispered when he released her lips.

The throaty sound of his name inflamed him. Sweeping Kit into his arms, Logan settled her gently on the cool leather and covered her trembling body with his.

Kit's moist, parted lips were a lure Logan made no effort to resist. Refusing the demands of his clamoring body, he moved slowly, outlining her beautiful mouth with the tip of his tongue before seeking the sweetness inside.

Needing to know her, the texture of her, Logan shifted his body slightly, stroking his palm down her slender form from her arched throat to her narrow hips and long thighs, while his tongue set a rhythm evocative of a deeper possession.

Kit's fingers speared through the thick strands of his hair. Her long nails raked his scalp, sending shudders cascading erratically down the length of his spine. His breathing constricted, Logan hung on to his shredding control, but his restraint shattered at the soft, urgent sounds that reached his ears from deep in Kit's throat. Spurred by her pleasure purrs, he thrust his hips into hers in a silent confession of his voracious hunger for her.

Logan was so lost within the mist of sensual fog he failed to notice the sounds of activity in the wide hall beyond the study door. He was easing Kit's silky pullover up her body when the petulant sound of Laureen's voice pierced the sensual haze.

"Well where could Kit have disappeared to?" Laureen wailed in exasperation. "Her father wants her to cut the first slice of her graduation cake."

Every tautened muscle in Logan's body froze into hard stillness as he relinquished the sweetness of Kit's mouth.

There was a murmuring response to Laureen from a voice Logan didn't recognize, then Laureen's reply rang clearly through the room.

"But why would Kit go back in the water?"

There came another murmured response, then Laureen cried, "We've got to find her. Bruce is getting impatient."

Sanity shuddered through Logan with the force of a blow to the stomach—and with it self-disgust. For a long instant he stared into Kit's passion-clouded eyes, then he thrust himself away from her and the sofa, the words *graduation cake* hammering in his mind.

Kit, his beloved Kit was seventeen, *seventeen*! And he had come to within moments of... Logan drew a harsh, ragged breath and turned away from the adult lure of her young eyes.

"Logan?" Kit made no attempt to disguise the confusion and hurt she felt at his sudden withdrawal.

Logan couldn't force himself to look at her; he'd known he couldn't trust himself that far.

"They're looking for you," Logan said roughly. "You'd better get yourself together and get out there."

"But..." Kit began tremulously.

"There are no buts, Kit." Knowing he had to shake her out of the sensual stupor, yet hating himself for doing it, Logan swung around to pin her with a gem-hard gaze. "I wanted to give you an example of how very vulnerable you are, brat." Logan's throat closed over the term. "You said you could handle pretty boy, but that was only because he *is* little more than a boy. I wanted to show you how very helpless you'd be in an encounter with a man." Logan felt more sick to his stomach with each succeeding lie that growled from his mouth.

Kit blinked rapidly, ineffectually, against the tears that brightened her eyes. Logan ground his teeth together and curled his hands into tight fists to control the urge to go to her, hold her, comfort her.

"You-you didn't really want me?" The note of pleading anguish in Kit's tone was almost his undoing.

"A man wants a woman, Kit," Logan lied through gritted teeth. "And you've got one helluva lot of growing up to do." The sound of Kit's sob was like a blade through Logan's chest.

"Do you hate me, Logan? Are you ashamed of me?"

Dear God, get her out of here, before I damn myself completely. The supplication was a cry straight from Logan's soul.

"I could never hate you, Kit. And I'm not ashamed of you." *I'm ashamed of me,* Logan told her silently. "Like Zack, I'll always be here for you. Now run along, your guests are waiting for you to slice the cake."

Logan had not tasted the cake that had been fashioned in the shape of a graduate's cap. He hadn't even seen the first slice into the elaborate confection. By the time the group had greeted a partially composed Kit, Logan had been on his way back to Nevada.

Damn!

Shifting his angular body uncomfortably on the curved couch, Logan opened his eyes and stared blankly at the open-beamed, cathedral-style ceiling.

He was sweating. His muscles were quivering. His blunt lashes were spiked and glistening with moisture. Logan was not unfamiliar with his mental or physical condition. He suffered the symptoms at regular intervals—usually upon waking from an erotic dream about Kit. The condition had endured for over eight years.

Eight years. Logan sighed. He had spent eight long years trying to deny an absolute. He had used other women deliberately, if compassionately, in an attempt to repudiate that absolute, and he had failed. Regardless how lovely, how willing, how *talented*, the woman of the moment, the reality of her had never been strong enough to erase the image of Kit.

As his body cooled and the tremors subsided, Logan blinked the stinging moisture from his eyes and nodded once, decisively. The love he felt for Kit was all-encompassing and consuming. It would not go away, never fade. He had eight years of solid proof.

And, damn it, why shouldn't Logan love Kathryn?

Pushing himself from the couch, Logan began unbuttoning his shirt as he walked to his bedroom with sure, purposeful strides.

After being closed up for over two weeks, the condo Kit had inherited from her father along with the casino seemed chilled and stuffy.

It was not yet sundown, hours earlier than she usually got home, when Kit let herself into the elegant apartment. The phone rang as she shut the door behind her. Frowning, she hurried to the delicate secretaire the gold-filigree French-style phone rested upon. Hoping to hear Logan's low voice, Kit was nonetheless not disappointed to recognize Thack's soft Texas drawl.

"Hi, honey. I just called to make sure you got back to Tahoe in one piece."

"I arrived safe and sound." Kit laughed. "Are you and Barbara in Palm Springs?" They had all departed from her brother's complex on the Big Sur at the same time; Zack and Aubrey to fly to Pennsylvania; his twin Thack and his wife, Barbara, to spend a week at the large house in Palm Springs; and Kit to Nevada and the casino—and Logan.

"Yeah." Thack chuckled. "This ain't no shack, honey. Barb's already declared she's in love."

"Barbara's welcome there each and every day of the year," Kit assured her half brother sincerely. "You both are."

"Like hell!" Thack exclaimed on a burst of laughter. "I appreciate the sentiment behind the invitation, but I've got a ranch to run in Texas."

Since he had brought up the subject, Kit willingly pursued it. "Thack, the sentiment is not implied, it is stated. I'm thoroughly delighted with my new brother and his wife."

"Thanks, Kit, we kind'a like you, too." Thack's voice was husky. "You and Zack and Aubrey."

Zack and Aubrey. Thack and Barbara. Kit and . . . Kit. She swallowed the sigh the thought produced, and went on in a controlled tone.

"The, ah, shack is well stocked, but if you need anything at all, don't hesitate to ask. I'm as close as the phone."

"Will do, honey, but I doubt we'll pine for anything," he assured her. Then his tone became brisk. "Did you have an opportunity to talk to either Logan McKittrick or Flint Falcon yet?"

Since Kit had discussed her business with both her brothers during her visit to the coast, Thack was completely apprised of her eagerness to sell the casino. He knew that she had a prospective buyer, a rather intimidating man named Flint Falcon. Thack was also aware of her frustration over Logan's hesitation about selling at all.

"I didn't talk to Mr. Falcon," Kit said. "But I saw Logan for a few minutes." She shivered from the memory of those minutes, especially the very last. "He still thinks it would be a mistake to sell."

"Well, from what you've told me about Logan, I think the man's got his head on straight," Thack observed. "I'm not sure about this Falcon character. I think I'll see what I can find out about him when I get home. I don't think I like the idea of my sister hanging out in a casino with hard cases."

Hard cases! Kit started to laugh, then sobered as an image of Flint Falcon's dark-skinned, blade-thin face rose in her mind. Having talked several times with the hard-faced, yet soft-spoken man, Kit knew instinctively that he was capable of ruthlessness. Then she did laugh as the content of Thack's statement registered.

"Oh, spare me!" she gurgled. "I didn't get another brother, I acquired another protector."

"You got it, honey," Thack drawled, then added, seriously, "Hey, keep in touch—right?"

"Yes, Thack. Enjoy your week at the house, and give my love to Barbara."

Kit slipped out of her jacket as she turned away from the desk. She had taken three steps when the phone rang again. It wasn't Logan this time, either. It was the man she'd moments ago discussed with her brother.

"I tried to reach you at the Silver Lining," Flint Falcon said in the tone Kit had secretly labeled "deadly quiet." "Mike Harmon informed me that you'd left for the day."

"Yes," Kit agreed to the obvious. "How are you, Mr. Falcon?"

"I'm fine, thank you," he responded softly. "And you?"

"Fine." Kit couldn't suppress the smile that curved her lips; Flint Falcon was always scrupulously polite.

"Have you given any more thought to my offer, Ms. Aimsley?" By his inflectionless voice, one could believe Flint Falcon didn't care one way or the other. Kit knew better. In her estimation, Falcon wanted the casino so badly he could taste it—which suited her. She wanted to get rid of it almost as badly.

"Yes, I have," she admitted, "and I believe it more than fair. But Mr. McKittrick is playing the proverbial fly. I'm still willing to sell you my seventy-five percent, though," she added hopefully.

"Sorry." Falcon didn't sound in the least sorry. "I want it all, or nothing. When can I meet with Mr. McKittrick?"

"Well, he was here in Tahoe this afternoon," Kit said. "But he gave me no indication of how long he was planning to stay." She gnawed on her lip a moment. "Suppose you call me in the office tomorrow morning, say around ten. In the meantime, I'll see if I can contact him. Will that do?"

"Yes." Stoic acceptance laced his soft voice. "I'm sorry if I disturbed you. Have a good evening, Ms. Aimsley."

After bidding Falcon good-night, Kit replaced the phone and turned from the desk. She had barely taken one step when the instrument shrilled again. Muttering "I don't believe this!" Kit snatched up the receiver.

"Yes!" she snapped.

"Touchy, aren't we?" Logan asked in a startled tone.

"I don't know about you," Kit retorted. "But I am. You are the third caller I've had since I walked in the door thirty minutes ago."

There was an instant of quiet, then Logan observed, "Popularity does have its price."

"I know—you exacted your measure in my office today," Kit reminded him. "I'm certainly glad I'm not quite that popular with everybody." She brought her free hand up to press her fingers against her lips.

"Kit—" Logan's tone became tense "—I'm sorry about that...incident. I want to talk to you about it."

Oh, no. Kit shook her head. She had been forced, by her youth as well as circumstances, to listen to him eight years ago. But she was no longer a shivering teenager. Kit caught a glimpse of her trembling fingers. Well, she was no longer a teenager.

"And I want to talk to you," she said sharply. "One of my callers was Mr. Falcon. He asked to meet with you. I told him I'd try to contact you. He's calling tomorrow at ten. Will you agree to at least talk to him?"

"Yes," Logan answered without hesitation. "If you'll agree to at least talk to me."

"That's blackmail, Logan McKittrick!" Kit admonished.

"Whatever it takes, Kathryn Aimsley," Logan retaliated.

Kit sighed and pressed her hand over her stomach. "When?" she asked tiredly, resigning herself to his big-brother lecture.

"Over dinner?" Logan had the grace to make it a request, not a demand.

Might as well get it over with, Kit thought wearily. Perhaps if Logan were allowed to get his harangue off his chest, and mind, he'd be in a better frame of mind when meeting Flint Falcon. One could always hope.

"All right, Logan," Kit agreed softly. "What time?"

"Would seven be convenient?"

"Seven would be fine."

Kit stared at the elegant ivory-and-gold phone long after she'd cradled the receiver. After the almost brutal kiss Logan had left her with earlier, the last thing she needed was lecture number four on the proper deportment of young ladies. She'd heard it all before—from both Logan and Zack.

The colors of the phone blurred as she narrowed her eyes. Simmering anger stiffened her spine.

"Damn it!" Kit muttered the words aloud.

She wasn't a kid anymore. Zack had ceased with the corrective, brotherly advice years ago. Kit's head snapped up as a realization hit her. She'd have laughed if Zack *had* tried the wiser, older brother routine! Where was it etched in stone that she had to listen to *anything* Logan McKittrick had to say?

Spinning away from the desk, Kit stormed into her lavender and silver bedroom. As she took off her clothes, she let memory spin in her mind. In that memory was a young Kit, cowering as she lay trembling on the leather sofa in her father's study, cringing inside as Logan's words hit her like individual blows.

Standing under a pulsating shower, Kit raised her hot face to the stinging spray of water.

Damned if she hadn't cowered that afternoon, too! Was she stupid or what? Kit asked herself scathingly, twisting the tap off with unnecessary force.

She was twenty-five years old, and not getting any younger. How long was she planning to wait for *old*—thirty-eight-year-old—Logan to wake up to the fact that she was all grown up?

Maybe what *old* Logan needed was a dose of his own brand of medicine.

The idea stopped Kit cold in the process of dressing. Her eyes gleamed sapphire bright as the idea expanded. Absently finishing with her clothes and makeup, Kit brushed her long, straight silvery hair to a sheen as she formulated a plan.

There had been several women in Logan's life that Kit knew of over the previous eight years. But, to the best of her knowledge, he had not been seeing any one particular woman for at least six months.

Fastening a slim gold watch on her wrist, Kit noted the time with a feline smile. It was six-fifty-seven, and Logan would be arriving momentarily. He was rarely, if ever, late for an appointment.

Swinging out of the bedroom, Kit fairly danced to the door when the doorbell pealed. As she opened the door she gazed, wide-eyed and all innocence, into Logan's somber countenance.

Oh, yes. Judging by his expression, Logan was prepared to render lecture number four—and possibly even five and six.

Lowering her lashes to conceal the gemlike glitter in her blue eyes, Kit swished by him into the corridor.

But, she wondered, was Logan prepared to be seduced?

Three

The fragrance of the vanilla-scented candle flickering inside a ruby-red, cut-glass bowl blended with the aroma of exquisite cuisine. The murmur of conversation from the surrounding tables heightened the sense of isolation. The large, elegant dining room was comfortably warm.

Kit's feet were getting colder by the second.

Toying with the long stem of her wineglass, Kit gazed quickly at Logan then, just as quickly, she glanced away. Deciding to seduce the formidable-looking man was one thing, actually *doing* it was something else altogether. Kit didn't know where to begin.

There was an aura about Logan that was rather off-putting, she mused, sliding her fingertips the length of the slender glass stem. Having never attempted seduction before, Kit wasn't sure if she could launch a successful campaign to entrance one of the ordinary men she knew, let alone Logan McKittrick.

And now, after their delicious meal had been finished, Kit's feeling of defeat increased with each passing minute. The only positive thing that had come from their dinner conversation was Logan's reluctant agreement to meet with Flint Falcon. In fact, the conversation had been so desultory that Logan hadn't even gotten around to his lecture.

"Dessert, Kit?"

Logan's soft inquiry shattered Kit's introspection. She glanced up, smothering a sigh with a smile.

"No, thank you." Some seductress you are, Kit berated herself. Why hadn't she responded enticingly, *"Yes, I'll have you for dessert, thank you"*? A smile teased the corners of her lips; the response sounded girlishly silly, even uttered silently.

"Coffee? A liqueur?" Logan persisted.

Kit started to shake her head, then caught herself sharply. Where *is* your mind, dummy? This is your opening—go for it!

"I'd like both," she murmured in what she hoped was a sensual tone. "But not here." Kit smiled—suggestively?

"No? Where, then?" No question was necessary about whether sensuousness or suggestiveness was woven through Logan's tone—his voice was loaded with both. His lips quirked appealingly. "Your place or mine?"

Oh, my, Kit moaned silently. The oldest invitation going and *her* breathing process goes haywire!

"To the point." Kit flashed a brilliant smile and missed the flare of intense interest in Logan's eyes. "Unoriginal, but to the point." Raising her glass she tossed off the last of her wine with a panache she was far from feeling. "My place," Kit said quickly, before she could change her mind.

Imitating Kit, Logan lifted his glass and drained it. His smile was very masculine and very wicked as he set the glass on the table decisively.

"Let's get out of here." Scraping his chair back, Logan got to his feet then circled the table to assist Kit. "I'm ready for, ah, coffee," he murmured as she rose.

A tingle of anticipation tiptoed down Kit's spine at the hint of sensuality in the deep timbre of his voice. What had Logan almost said before changing the word to coffee? she wondered, preceding him from the restaurant.

In the big estate wagon, nervous and filled with trepidation, Kit raked her mind for a subject, any subject, that would ease the tension that suddenly hummed between them like an exposed electrical wire. When every topic that came to mind seemed pedestrian and banal, she fell back on the second love of her life, Logan's ranch.

"Did you complete whatever it was that was keeping you so busy at the ranch a few weeks ago?" she asked overbrightly, inwardly wincing at the nervous crackle in her voice.

"Umm," Logan hummed, not at all forthcoming.

Wonderful. Kit sighed. Well, now that the subject of the ranch has been effectively shot down in flames, where do we go from here? Do we talk about the weather? Kit smothered a giggle by clearing her throat.

"Are you catching a cold?" Logan asked sharply.

Not a cold—rampant idiocy. Kit bit back the flippant reply.

"No. I had a tickle in my throat."

"Better now?" Logan slanted a concerned glance at her.

"Yes, fine," Kit hastened to assure him, then fell silent to search her mind for more conversational tidbits. Logan ended the silence this time.

"When I spoke to you earlier, you said I was your third caller. Besides Falcon, who else knew that you were back in Tahoe?"

"Thack," Kit replied, then immediately wondered if she should have attempted to pique his curiosity by being vague. Some hot temptress you are, she thought wryly.

"He's still at Zack's place in Big Sur?" Though Logan didn't take his gaze from the road, Kit saw the questioning arch of his right brow.

"No. He and Barbara left when I did. They're at the house in Palm Springs." A soft smile played over her lips. "They're still on their honeymoon."

"Very romantic," Logan observed caustically.

Now Kit was piqued. "Yes, it is." She shifted on the bench seat to face him. "You'd have to see Thack and Barbara together, Logan. They're so obviously in love, it's almost embarrassing to watch them."

"Hmm."

Kit glowered at him. She'd about had enough of the noncommittal "hmm."

"Which means exactly what?" she demanded.

Logan flashed a smile at her that Kit felt in every pulse point in her body. Behind the smile, Logan's mind was racing. Is that what Kit wants? he mused, carefully negotiating the car onto the ramp leading to the parking area beneath the condo. Does Kit want to be romanced?

"It means," he finally answered, "that I'm unsure of couples who make a show of their emotions." He sure as hell had never worn his heart on his sleeve.

"Thack and Barbara do not make a *show* of their emotions!" Kit scrambled from the car the moment Logan brought it to a stop. Annoyed with him, she didn't notice the glance he slid over her long legs when her skirt inched up as she shifted across the seat. "But the proof of the love they feel for each other is there every time they glance at one another," she said, striding angrily to the private elevator.

"Will you calm down?" Logan came up beside her at a leisurely pace. "What's all the fuss about, anyway?" Logan observed her closely as he followed her into the lift; maybe her answer would give him a clue as to how he should go about *romancing* her.

"I'll tell you what all the fuss is about!" As the lift ascended, Kit whirled to face him, hands planted on her slim hips. "You are such a darned cynic," she charged heatedly. "You always have been. The oh-so-independent, complete-unto-himself rancher observing the foibles of others from a secure position." Kit slowly perused his length with a frosty glance as the elevator doors swished open. Then she spun away to storm down the corridor to her apartment.

Stunned, Logan stood absolutely still. The movement of the automatic doors as they began to close snapped him into action. Halting the doors with one broad palm, he stepped from the car, then slowly trailed in Kit's wake along the wide hallway.

Was that how he was perceived by others? Logan shook his head wonderingly. Did he really appear cold and emotionless—a cynical bystander to life's passing parade?

Ha! Logan's lips twisted. If they only knew. If *Kit* only knew! Cold? His blood ran like liquid fire through his veins. Emotionless? He was a jangled mass of conflicting emotions. A cynical observer? Well, perhaps, Logan conceded. But there were reasons for his attitude, and every one of those reasons was tied to the forbidden feelings he'd harbored for Kit for nearly nine years.

Hell, Logan thought, hesitating at the open door to Kit's apartment. It was damned lucky he hadn't gone off the deep end long ago, considering his mental state.

"Are you coming in?" Kit demanded irritably from the living room. "Or were you planning to have your coffee out there in the hallway?"

Coffee? Logan scowled fiercely as he crossed the threshold and shut the door. What he needed was a drink—a stiff drink. Damn! Kit had lobbed a monkey wrench into his plans for an *at home* romantic evening!

As Logan moved into the room, Kit walked out, heading for the narrow, utilitarian kitchen. Scowl in place, he ambled in her wake.

"By your definition, I'm pretty much of a small-minded bastard," Logan muttered, leaning against the counter where she was fussing with the automatic coffee maker.

Kit carefully poured the water into the top of the machine before turning to look him directly in the eyes.

"I never said you were small-minded."

Logan's tight lips lost the battle against a smile. "But pretty much of a bastard?" He arched one dark brow.

Kit smiled, saccharine-sweet. "If you insist."

Logan contemplated her annoyed expression a few minutes, then sighed. "You're still ticked about that kiss in your office this afternoon, aren't you?"

Kit widened her eyes in feigned surprise. "Was that what that was? Well, silly me! I *assumed* it was a kiss, but when you smacked it on me, I wasn't quite sure."

Logan shifted uncomfortably. Kit's charge was too close to the mark for comfort. In truth, he hadn't been in complete control that afternoon for a multitude of reasons, all of them having to do with the jealousy raging inside him. And the worst part was that he had no proof that the jealousy was founded in fact, and no right to feel jealous even if his fears were true.

"I'd never hit you, brat, and you know it."

"Oh, I know you'd never swing at me with your fist or even your open palm." Kit turned back to the coffee maker to stare at the thin stream of coffee trickling into the glass pot. "But you have no compunction at all about hitting me with your sarcasm, *or* that detested nickname, 'brat,' *or* even this afternoon's display that you dare call a kiss." Whipping around, she glared at him. "I sincerely hope you weren't planning on making a habit of those kisses."

Staring at her through eyes shaded to jade with bleakness, Logan was assaulted by emotions that ran the gamut from frustration to admiration. To him, Kit was always beautiful. But, in anger, Kit was one magnificent woman.

One magnificent woman. The phrase took root in Logan's mind. Sketching the shimmering highlights in her silvery hair, he felt a twist in his gut, followed by the sting of his conscience. The sting seared like a branding iron as his gaze drifted over her delicate features before sweeping down her rounded, enticing form.

No doubt about it, he concluded as his hungry gaze returned to her expressionless face, Kit was most assuredly a woman.

"Coffee's ready."

Logan straightened away from the counter as Kit took two translucent china cups from the cabinet above the countertop. Understanding came as he silently watched her spare, graceful movements preparing a tray to carry into the living room.

With new insight, Logan realized that his problem stemmed from his failure to recognize Kit's growth, both physically and intellectually. Subconsciously he'd continued to think of her as the immature teenager she'd been the night of her graduation party.

"Coming?" Her slender body still taut with anger, Kit swung away from the counter and marched into the living room.

Grasping the tray loaded with a coffeepot, cups, a small china creamer and a bottle of brandy he hadn't even noticed Kit take from the cabinet, Logan again trailed after her.

Their conversation every bit as desultory as it had been earlier in the restaurant, they drank their coffee and brandy in an atmosphere of constraint, both grappling with their own thoughts.

Hopeless, the whole idea was utterly hopeless, Kit decided, swallowing a groan with a sip of brandy. *Logan will never think of me as anything other than his little sister, to be indulged, protected and occasionally chastised. The plan of seduction is no longer viable—if it really ever had been!*

Although Kit had never before contemplated seducing a man—let alone attempting it—she felt positive the object of her machinations would first have to regard her as a mature woman. He'd have to consider her an equal, someone who was fully aware of her actions, and the possible—no probable—results of them.

So, then, the first order of business was to convince Logan of her maturity and equality. Terrific. To Kit, the task before her appeared about as simple as navigating the Pacific on a raft.

She considers me in the same vein as she does Zack and Thackery—an older brother, Logan reflected, refilling the fragile cup he'd emptied with two long swallows. *And with excellent reason. Till now, that's exactly what I have been. Suitors come in the form of equals, not authority figures.*

Logan saw his path clearly. What he had to do was get Kit to think of him as a man—and not one of the brother variety. Wonderful. Logan grimaced into the dainty cup. Maybe his path was clearly delineated, but it sure as hell had its emotional hazards.

"Logan—"

"Kit—"

They spoke in unison, then fell silent, staring warily at each other across the small space that separated their chairs.

Logan smiled faintly. "Go ahead. What were you going to say?"

Kit hesitated, then blurted starkly, "I think it's time for you to accept that I'm a competent adult."

Logan laughed softly, shaking his head at the flare of anger that leaped into her bright eyes. "I'm not laughing at you, honey," he said with firm assurance. "I'm amused by the situation."

"Why don't you explain exactly what you mean?" Kit retorted, obviously unconvinced. "Then maybe we can both laugh." She paused, then added, "And don't call me 'honey' in that tone. It sounds condescending."

"It wasn't meant to," Logan murmured. "And the explanation's simple. I had just decided it was time I treated you as a person, and not a sister." His lips curved sardonically. "If you know what I mean?"

Kit's pent-up breath whooshed out of her body on a long sigh. Her smile was a reflection of his. "Isn't it strange?" she mused, choosing her words slowly. "We know each other so well, and yet not at all."

"Yeah." Logan nodded, solemnly. "Maybe we've been standing too close to get an objective view."

"You mean, like not being able to see the forest for the trees?" Kit asked, only half joking.

"Exactly." Logan nodded again, briefly but firmly. "Instead of big brother, little sister, perhaps it's time we got to know Kit and Logan." A smile lifted the corners of his lips. "Who knows, we might even like each other."

"We might at that." Kit returned the smile. "And how do you suggest we go about this experiment of getting to know one another?"

Logan opened his mouth to speak, then closed it again. In theory, it sounded easy. In practice, it wasn't. As Kit had pointed out, they *did* know each other— and yet they didn't. A frown drew his dark brows together, giving him a fierce look. Damned if Kit wasn't right on the mark, he mused, staring into her expectant face. He knew the forest like a native, but the individual trees were an unknown to him.

Standing abruptly, Logan extended his right hand as he leaned toward her.

"The name's Logan McKittrick," he said in all seriousness. "And you are?" he asked politely.

For an instant Kit looked startled, then her blue eyes began to gleam with amusement. Controlling her expression, she rose gracefully to her feet and placed her palm against his.

"I'm Kathryn Aimsley, Mr. McKittrick." A warm, impersonal smile tilted her lips. "And it's a pleasure to meet you..." The smile escaped her control to slip into a grin as she added, "I hope."

"Knock it off," Logan scolded sternly, fighting a battle with his own twitching lips. "This is serious business here." He applied gentle pressure to her fingers before releasing her hand. Straightening to his full six feet, he ran an assessing glance over her slender form.

Her hand tingling from his touch, Kit met Logan's emerald-green gaze when it returned to her face. "Well?" she prompted.

"You're a beautiful woman, Kathryn Aimsley," he said in a subdued tone.

Kit felt a jolt of sheer pleasure snake through her at his softly spoken compliment. Wetting her suddenly parched lips, she smiled tremulously. "Thank you, Mr. McKittrick."

"Logan," he corrected her in a murmur. "May I call you Kathryn?"

"My family and friends call me Kit," she said, clenching her fingers to contain the tremors rippling down her arms.

"I know." Logan's tone was low, and as dark as a shuttered bedroom. "That's why I'd prefer to call you Kathryn."

Kit's mouth and throat went bone dry at the sensuous note in his voice and the smoldering light in the depths of his green eyes. This was a Logan she had only glimpsed for a few mind-shattering seconds eight years ago. And, though he was the same Logan she had loved all her life, he was different—excitingly different. The difference made Kit feel weak in every muscle in her body.

"I... I rather like the sound of Kathryn," she finally managed to answer, sinking back onto her chair. "Won't you sit down, Logan?" Gazing up at him, she indicated the coffee tray absently. "Would you like a cup of coffee?" she went on, as if unaware that he'd drunk two cups of the brew mere minutes before.

"No, thank you." Logan moved his head negatively, then skimmed a molten gaze the length of her that she felt in the exact center of her being. "I doubt that coffee can quench the thirst building inside me."

"Ahhh...thirst?" Kit, now Kathryn, squeaked.

Logan's lips curved, not cynically but sardonically. "C'm'on, Kathryn. Walk me to the door."

What was this? Kit stared at him in blank astonishment. "You're leaving?"

Logan nodded sharply. "I think I'd better." He turned away with obvious reluctance. "We just met—remember?" He glanced at her over his broad shoulder as he sauntered to the door.

"But—" Realizing that he was really set on going, Kit scrambled to her feet and rushed to where he stood, hand poised over the doorknob. "But, Logan," she protested. "I thought we were going to get to know each other better!" She gazed up at him beseechingly. "Why are you leaving now?"

Logan's smile was loaded with derision, all aimed at himself. "Because, Kathryn," he murmured, bending to her, "I want to kiss you." His eyes narrowed over a flare of desire when she softly gasped. "No, that's a lie," he went on roughly, bringing his hand up to brush his fingers along the outline of her trembling mouth. "I want to eat you alive."

A low moan whispered through Kit's lips. His mouth was so close, so very close to her own she could almost taste it. At that instant she knew exactly what he was feeling; her own lips burned with the desire to explore every inch of his tanned, muscular body.

"Logan." His name whimpered off the tip of her tongue as she moistened her lips.

The muscles over Logan's stomach clenched into tight knots. He had decided not to touch her, not yet, not until she knew him, the real him, better. Yet the yearning sound of her voice as she whimpered his name, the enticing glide of her tongue as she wet her lips, drove the decision right out of his mind. Just one kiss, he vowed to himself as he lowered his head. Just one sweet kiss to make up for that afternoon.

Logan's lips touched Kit's like the gentle blessing of spring rain. And, like the parched earth, he drank from her mouth, at first gratefully, then, with ever-increasing hunger as his body hardened with long suppressed need. The taste of her was everything he remembered, yet new, exciting, wildly arousing. As a teenager, Kit had been as tempting as the blush on an early peach. Now her taste was more of the mature, ripened exotic fruit, juices close to the surface, ready to bathe the senses with the first hungry bite.

Famished from self-denial, Logan nibbled greedily on Kit's willing lips, caressing the tender flesh before slipping his warm tongue inside the delicious hot moistness of her mouth.

Kit's arms circled his waist at the same instant his arms enfolded her slender form, crushing her rounded softness to the hardened angles of his body. Splaying one hand at the base of her spine, he lifted her up into the heat of him, while his other hand tangled in the silky strands of her hair.

Feeling light-headed, almost faint, Kit clung to Logan's waist, instinctively arching her hips into alignment with his. There was a world of difference between the way Logan was now kissing her and the kiss he'd bruised her lips with earlier that day. This kiss was even worlds different from the kisses he'd given her on the night of her graduation party. This open-mouth, passionate kiss was both reverent and ravishing. Kit responded to the life-renewing heat of

Logan's kiss like a wilting flower opening to the blessing of warm sun rays.

"No." The whispered protest was torn from her throat when Logan lifted his mouth from hers.

"I must go." Even as he spoke, Logan lowered his head to the gentle curve of her throat, seeking the vulnerable arch of satiny skin.

Shivering at the sensations caused by the motion of his parted lips against her skin, Kit raked his broad back lightly with her nails, digging in reflexively when his teeth nipped her shouler.

"Ooooh, Logan!" Kit could barely breathe for the heat rising in waves through her body. She ached, in her breasts, in her limbs, in her loins. "Logan!" The cry was wrenched from her as his hand closed over one tingling breast.

"I told you," he muttered, skimming his lips up her throat and over her jaw to the corner of her mouth. "I want to eat you alive."

Yes! Kit didn't have time to voice her eager acceptance, for his mouth slid over hers, taking her breath and rattling her senses.

"One more kiss, Ki—" He caught himself and Kit could almost hear the smile in his voice. "Kathryn," he breathed excitingly. "Just one more, then I've got to get out of here—or I won't be able to."

Kit's restless, searching hands skimmed his ribs, then slid up his chest, fingernails scoring the silky material of his shirt. Logan grunted as the tip of one nail scraped a hard, flat nipple. His reaction thrilled her, instilled a need to investigate the broad plane of his chest. But, even as her hands moved to the shirt buttons, Logan's mouth crashed down on hers. The driving hunger of his lips scattered her senses, and Kit curled her arms around his corded neck to keep herself from crumbling to her knees.

The quality of Logan's kiss had once again changed. Raw need was the force behind the lips that moved urgently on Kit's, and the tongue that scoured the deepest reaches of her mouth.

Spearing her fingers into his hair, Kit shivered from the sensation created by the vibrant strands gliding against the sensitive skin between her fingers.

Weak and quivering with a need growing stronger inside her with each passing second, Kit gave herself in untamed abandonment to his silent demand for full participation in the kiss. Arching compulsively, she molded her body to the hard male form curving over her.

The groan that vibrated in Logan's throat was a sweet musical symphony to Kit's ears. Tightening her hold, she grasped his hair and tugged, not in a bid for freedom but in a plea for an even deeper intimacy. Boldly, she stroked his tongue with hers, reveling in the shudder that rippled the length of his tall frame.

Logan's consuming kiss went on forever, and ended much too soon. A string of harshly muttered curses sounded loud in the sudden stillness as Logan tore his mouth from hers.

Shocked, Kit stared into his passion-clouded eyes.

"I'm sorry." Stepping back, away from her, Logan raked shaky fingers through the thick strands of his auburn hair.

His abrupt action and roughly uttered apology jolted through Kit, bringing reality back with a chilling rush. What was he apologizing for? she wondered bleakly, gazing at him from eyes suddenly bright with the sting of tears. Was Logan sorry for the kiss or the curse?

"Don't look like that!" Logan's tone was stark with self-condemnation. "Kathryn, please. Don't look at me like that!"

Kit blinked rapidly. "Like what?" she asked in a dry croak, shivering at his touch when he grasped her arms.

"Like you're going to cry." His fingers flexed, digging spasmodically into the soft flesh of her upper arms. "Like you've been wounded." His features tightened, locking into a hard mask. "Like you've been emotionally injured."

"I'm not going to cry," Kit said huskily, denying the moisture spiking her long, pale blond lashes. "And I don't feel wounded or injured in any way." Drawing a deep breath, she met his narrow-eyed stare directly. "What I'm feeling is a sense of confusion and rejection," she dared to admit.

"Rejection!" Logan exclaimed, his facial mask shattering into astonishment. "After the way I just kissed you? How the hell can you be feeling rejected?"

"But you immediately apologized for that kiss," she reminded him tremulously, blinking against a fresh surge of tears.

"And that's why you're also confused?" His lips tilted with the hint of a smile, Logan slowly drew her unresisting body into a gentle embrace.

"Yes." Kit buried her face in the curve of his neck, inhaling the spicy, male scent that was uniquely Logan.

"Foolish woman." Logan rubbed his cheek against her silky hair. "I apologized for swearing," he murmured. "And I swore because I didn't want to let you go, didn't want the kiss to end."

"I didn't either," Kit admitted artlessly.

Logan's arms tightened, crushing her to him. "But I had to end it, and I've got to get out of here." His lips brushed her temple. "Because if I don't leave now, we're going to wind up in bed together." Releasing her with obvious reluctance, Logan again stepped back, away from the lure of her wide eyes and kiss-reddened lips.

"Logan?" Kit's tone was unsteady from renewed sensual arousal. "Would winding up in bed together be so very wrong?"

A spark flared to a dark green flame in his eyes. "Wrong? No, Kathryn, it could never be wrong." The flame in Logan's eyes began to dance teasingly as he shook his head slowly. "But it would be bad timing," he suggested. "We just met each other—remember?" Smiling, he again reached for the doorknob. "I certainly don't want you to get the wrong impression of me."

"Wrong impression?" Kit frowned. "What do you mean?"

"Why, that I'm more interested in your body," he teased, swinging the door open, "than your mind."

Four

The smile of bemusement curving Kit's lips remained intact for all of fifty-five seconds after Logan quietly closed the door. Her expression dreamy, Kit crossed the room and was bending to collect the coffee tray when a thought intruded, chasing the smile from her lips and the dreamy expression from her face.

Had Logan meant his parting statement as a dig? Despite his teasing tone, had he intended to remind her of the man who *had* been more interested in her body than her mind?

Distracted, Kit straightened and turned, forgetting the coffee tray as she slowly walked to her bedroom.

Embarrassed, shamed by her own behavior, Kit had deeply buried the memory of the man and the circumstances surrounding the incident. Now remembrance rushed into her consciousness in full, living color, staining her cheeks pink as she recalled her impetuous actions.

The incident had begun innocently enough. Less than a month had passed since her graduation party and that shattering scene with Logan in her father's study. Determined not to live off her parents, and to prove herself an adult, Kit had auditioned for a minor part in a film being cast by an acquaintance of her father's. Though she'd been selected for the role over the dozen or so other young women who'd auditioned, Kit had the satisfaction of knowing that her reading had gained her the part, not any pressure applied by her father. In truth, Bruce Aimsley had been opposed to Kit being involved in any way, shape or form in the film industry; Bruce wanted Kit to go to college. Yet, with only her high school dramatics class performances as experience, Kit had won the small but meaty role of the ingenue.

Kit's father had not been the only member of the family to oppose her debut into film; Kit's brother Zack had nearly exploded, especially when it was revealed that the film was to be shot on location in the south of France.

"You're too young!" Zack had stated with that infuriating *older brother* resolve.

"I'll be eighteen in a few months!" Kit had countered hotly.

"Which is still too young to go traipsing off to France by yourself," Bruce had said, agreeing with his stepson's objection.

"But I won't *be* by myself!" Kit had argued, her tone shrill with frustration. "I'll be with the entire film company, for heaven's sake!"

The bitter argument raged until the week before the film crew was due to depart for France. Unhappy, torn between wanting to please her father and brother and needing to assert herself, Kit was on the verge of capitulation when her mother intervened, ending the tempest with her own inimitable brand of convoluted logic.

"But of course Kit's going to France!" Laureen exclaimed, as if becoming aware of the altercation at that moment. "I've made appointments for her to have fittings for a new wardrobe with the top Paris designer!" She waved her slender hand dismissively when Bruce and Zack began to object. "Kit will be perfectly safe. I've asked my friend, Jenene, to look after her."

"Jenene lives in Paris!" Bruce barked.

"But she has a château in the district the film is being set in," Laureen retorted serenely.

Kit had departed with the film crew and, though she did have tea with her mother's friend one warm afternoon in Paris, she hadn't set eyes on Jenene again throughout her stay in France. Indeed, it wouldn't have mattered if the matronly Jenene *had* moved her entire household to her château. By her second week at the film site, Kit had been ensnared in the web woven by the man who'd been cast in the second male lead.

Absently undressing for bed, Kit winced as an image of the ambitious actor focused in her mind's eye. Uncharacteristically ignoring her clothes lying in a heap on the carpet, Kit slipped between the sheets, attempting to banish the man's visage by shutting her eyes tightly. When it became obvious that her ploy wasn't going to work, she resigned herself to the flow of memories.

His name was Drake Boltz, which was unimportant now since it no longer appeared on any screen credits and wasn't his real name to begin with. With his unruly long hair, smoldering dark eyes and sensuous, full, pouting lower lip, Drake was the breathing image of a screen anti-hero. It was really too bad he had absolutely no acting ability to go along with his looks. His true talent lay in the seduction of young women, the more innocent the better. And, within seconds of being introduced to her, he had directed his talent toward Kit.

Still smarting over Logan's ruthlessly administered *lesson*, Kit had responded to Drake's single-minded pursuit like a parched flower to warm spring rain. Eight years her senior, at twenty-six, Drake's already jaded senses were aroused by Kit's fresh young beauty and long-limbed, unaffected sensuality.

Wily and experienced, Drake read Kit as easily as an open book and planned his campaign accordingly. He spent every free minute with her, first offering friendship, then compassionate understanding, and finally affection without pressure. Not by word or action had Drake hinted that his goal was seduction.

Serenely unaware of the dark passion simmering under Drake's smooth surface, Kit blithely followed his lead . . . and came very close to losing both her innocence and self-respect.

Thrilled with being a member of the cast, and fascinated with the mechanics of making a movie, Kit worked harder than ever before in her life. When the work day was finally over, she basked in the undemanding attention of the brooding actor, whose every move was followed by avid, lustful feminine eyes.

Of course, Kit had no way of knowing that one of the females shrewdly monitoring Drake's every movement would murmur a warning into the ear of a man who was a friend of Bruce Aimsley's acquaintance in the film industry. The warning was transmitted to an office in Hollywood, then relayed to Bruce, who angrily repeated it to Zack, who related it to Logan.

At about the same time that Zack and Logan were boarding the Concorde in New York, Kit was celebrating the announcement of a long, work-free weekend. Drake had invited her to spend the unexpected holiday in the French Alps and she'd agreed, not knowing that the actor had decided it was time to close in for the kill.

Blissfully unaware of Drake's well-thought-out advance, Kit had just about convinced herself that she was in love with him. She had come to the conclusion somewhat resentfully, after finally resigning herself to the realization that Logan would forever regard her as his *little sister*, to be spoiled and protected, loved no less than an indulged sister, but no more either.

Laughing and chattering at an almost frenetic pace with several of the crew members she'd made friends with, Kit helped Drake stash their overnight cases into the small sports car he'd rented for their trip. Then, denying a growing sense of apprehension, she buckled herself into the bucket seat, smiled brilliantly, and gave a final wave as Drake set the car, and the conclusion of his well-formed plans, into motion.

Kit could hardly know that some two hours after their departure, a granite-faced Logan and an obviously furious Zack were grimly questioning those same crew members.

For Kit, life had become complicated very soon after their arrival in the tiny village Drake had chosen as the perfect spot for her initiation into the pleasures of physical sensuality....

Uncomfortable with her thoughts, Kit moved restlessly on her bed as the memories pounded ruthlessly against her consciousness. Unable to halt the rushing flow, she caught her lower lip between her teeth and stifled a sob of shame as she remembered the headstrong foolishness of her actions. Strangely, even though eight years had passed, every movement, every word spoken, came back as clearly as if the scene had been enacted that very day.

"Not hungry, Sweet?" Drake smiled across the table at Kit's bowed head.

"Ah...what?" Kit blinked and attempted to gather her chaotic thoughts—the uppermost being, What am I doing here?

Drake indicated her barely touched dinner with a slight nod. "You're not eating." His full lips curved appealingly, the tone of his voice teased. "Surely you're not nervous?" His dark eyebrows peaked attractively.

Kit fought a sinking sensation in her stomach. "Nervous?" she repeated, forcing a shaky laugh. "No! Of course not. I—I'm, umm—excited! I guess." Silently bemoaning the squeaky edge to her tone, she smiled brightly. "Why would I be nervous?"

"Why indeed?" Smooth as glass, Drake's voice skimmed across the table and seemed to slide down the length of her spine. "Then, since you're obviously finished, shall we take this bottle of wine and retire to our room?"

Staunchly refusing to acknowledge the shiver his tone produced along her spine as fear, Kit somehow managed to keep her smile in place. She wasn't quite as successful with keeping her voice steady.

"Yes." The agreement trembled from her dry lips. "We might as well—" Kit bit off the words "—get it over with."

As she preceded Drake up the dimly lit narrow staircase in the small inn, Kit could no longer deny the fear coalescing in her mind. Her trepidation increased as Drake shut the door, closing them inside the quaintly furnished bedroom that contained one large bed. The soft click of the lock being set rocketed through Kit with the force of a deafening explosion. Fear ballooned into stark terror.

Trying to appear casual, she glanced away from the self-satisfied expression settling on Drake's face and stared blankly through the lace-curtained window into the complete blackness of the night beyond the pane.

"Tired?"

Kit started at the low sound of Drake's voice close to her ear, and shivered when his hand touched her arm.

"No." In the same instant she murmured the denial, Kit wondered if she'd made a mistake. Had Drake been offering her a way out of this situation she was beginning to find intolerable? Would he have bid her a soft good-night and left her alone if she'd answered affirmatively? The caressing glide of Drake's hand as he slid it up her arm and along her shoulder gave an answer more eloquent than words; nothing would dissuade Drake this night.

"That's good." Drake's fingers lifted the fall of silvery hair at her nape; his lips brushed the vulnerable skin exposed. "We've got the entire night before us, sweet." Drake's moist lips found her tender earlobe; his teeth nibbled gently. Kit trembled, not with sensual arousal as he obviously thought, but with revulsion. "A night neither one of us will forget," he continued, his voice thickening.

Kit's fingers clenched as Drake's arms circled her waist, drawing her taut body back into the hardening muscles of his chest and thighs. He misread the gasp of protest that escaped her tight throat. Laughing softly, he slid his hand up to capture one small breast.

"So slim, so delicate," he whispered, his tone hoarse with growing passion. "And so very deliciously inexperienced." His touch less gentle, Drake turned her to him, crushing her quivering body to his.

"Drake!" The muffled cry was all Kit could manage before his open mouth clamped onto hers.

Logan! Kit's silent cry remained within her mind, reverberating over and over again as Drake's hungry mouth fed on her trembling lips. An image formed in response to her cry: an image of a tall, imposing, auburn-haired man with rugged features, chilling green eyes, and whose kiss had the power to sear a woman's soul.

And that's how Logan and Zack found her when Zack furiously kicked open the locked bedroom door.

"You son of a bitch!" Zack's voice was harsh with anger, his face frightening as he strode across the room to tear Kit from Drake's arms. "She's under age! Do you want to be charged with statutory rape?" he snarled.

As shaken as Kit was she understood why Zack had used the term "statutory". Though her brother seemed like a giant, blond, avenging angel, Kit realized that Zack was convinced of her complicity with Drake's seduction . . . and, to a certain extent, Zack's assumption was correct.

And yet it wasn't the sight and sound of her brother that kept Kit mute, shivering with reaction and burning with shame, while the usually smooth, urbane actor attempted to bluster his way out of trouble. It was the expression on Logan's face—or, more precisely, the absolute *absence* of expression there. Austere, withdrawn, Logan's green eyes were the only feature on his face that expressed any emotion, and those eyes froze Kit's spirit with their contempt.

Locked within Logan's cold, green blaze, Kit remembered little of the subsequent action as she was hustled away from the tiny inn. Only bits and fragments of Zack's scolding tirade echoed in her mind.

"I knew allowing you to come to France was a mistake!" he ranted, nearly throwing Kit into the back seat of the car he'd rented.

"It was not a mistake!" Kit hotly denied his assertion. "I love working on the film!"

"And that excuse for a man," Zack gritted, sliding onto the front seat, "I suppose you love him, too?"

Her face over-warm, her insides freezing, Kit stared at the broad, rigid back of the man sitting in con-

demning silence behind the steering wheel. Logan
hadn't uttered a sound since he and Zack had burst
into the room, but then, he hadn't had to murmur a
word; the emerald hardness of his eyes spoke reams
about his disappointment in her. At Zack's harsh
question, his glance sliced to the rearview mirror,
piercing Kit to the depths of her soul.

"I-I thought I was in love with him," she mumbled
miserably. Unable to meet Logan's stare, she lowered
her gaze to her tightly clasped hands. "He, uh, treated
me like a woman," she added in a whisper.

"Why the hell wouldn't he?" Zack demanded,
shifting in the seat to glare at her. "He wanted what a
woman could give him!" Kit could hear his teeth grind
together in frustration before he went on angrily,
"And you played right into his hands—didn't you?"

Shamed, yet still rebellious, Kit jerked her head up,
her delicate chin thrust forward defiantly. For an instant her hot gaze tangled with glittering green reflected in the mirror, then she shifted her glance to
challenge Zack's blazing stare. Feeling Logan's contempt to the marrow of her bones, no power on earth
could have forced Kit to answer in her own defense.

Let them think what they like, Kit told herself in
childish indignation, meeting Zack's gaze directly,
while feeling lacerated from the impact of Logan's.
Amazingly, her brother gave way first.

"Do you still fancy yourself in love with him?"
Zack sighed, unwittingly hurting her by allowing his
shoulders to slump in defeat.

From the corner of her eye, Kit noted that there
wasn't a hint of a slump in Logan's wide shoulders—
if anything, they appeared to square more firmly.

"No, I no longer *fancy* myself in love with Drake." Regret tinged Kit's subdued tone, regret for the irretrievable loss of Logan's unqualified approval. A sad smile curved her lips. "I couldn't love a man who wasn't even strong enough to stand up to my brother."

An instant of silence followed Kit's flippant statement, then the quiet was shattered by the sudden roar of the car's engine being brought abruptly to life.

In the distance, a corresponding roar of an obviously powerful sports car startled Kit from her memories of the past.

Bolting upright, she sat trembling in the silver glow that spilled into her bedroom from a three-quarter moon. A sharp pain speared through her chest as she drew a deep breath. Even after all these years, the memory had the power to inflict pain in her body as well as her conscience.

Raising her arm, Kit raked long fingers through the tangled strands of hair that gleamed like streaming rain in the whitish moonlight. A longing sigh whispered through her lips as her hand dropped limply into her lap.

What a complete and absolute idiot she'd made of herself, and what a fool she'd been trying to retaliate for what she had considered to be Logan's rejection of her as a woman. All she had accomplished was to prove to Logan and everybody else how very young and inexperienced she really was. For, mulishly entrenched within that lack of maturity, Kit had steadfastly refused to offer either an explanation or an apology for her behavior.

Kit's sniffle sounded loud in the quiet bedroom as hot tears slid silently down her cold cheeks. A wistful smile moved fleetingly over her lips, a smile of pity for the seventeen-year-old Kit who'd been too proud—and too obstinate—to admit to either her lack of judgment or her continued state of innocence. And so, caught within a cocoon of pride, Kit had watched the Logan she'd adored as a big brother, and come to love as a man, withdraw from her in disgust.

Made restless from her mental sojourn, Kit pushed back the bedcovers and slid from the bed. Pulling on her robe as she went, she drifted into the living room. A frown darkened her pale brow as her glance fell on the coffee tray. Sighing over her forgetfulness, Kit lifted the tray and walked into the kitchen, flicking the light switch on with a quick movement of her elbow.

After rinsing the cups and saucers, Kit stood irresolute at the sink, absently wiping the gleaming burnt-orange countertop with a moist dishcloth, recalling the results of her precipitous action with the actor-would-be-seducer. The scene after Kit, Logan and Zack had returned to the flat she shared with two other girls came to mind.

"I'm under contract, I must finish the film!" Kit had argued when Zack declared he was taking her home immediately.

"The hell with the contract," he'd muttered dismissively. "I'm not leaving you here alone."

Kit had been reduced to pleading. "Zack, please. There are only a few weeks left till wrap-up. I'll be perfectly alright." Kit had regretted the words of assurance the instant they'd sprung from her trembling lips.

Zack's had superior look deepened her regret. "Why does that refrain sound so familiar?" he'd wondered aloud, arching a gold-blond eyebrow at the silently but watchful Logan.

"From an old song, maybe?" The coolly drawled question had marked the first time Logan had spoken. Looking straight at Zack, Logan hadn't bothered to spare as much as a glance for Kit.

That particular moment had proved a turning point for Kit. In a gesture more telling than a spate of angrily flung invectives, she had turned her back on the two men she had spent her young life trying to please. Striding over to the window, she had stared out at the impossibly beautiful view of the Mediterranean coastline.

After a few seconds of reflection, Kit bit her lip and squared her shoulders. Determination radiated from her tall, slender frame.

"I am not breaking my contract," she enunciated slowly. "Nor will I allow you to buy it out," she added, crushing Zack's offer even as he opened his mouth to make it. Turning, she carefully avoided Logan's eyes by gazing directly at her brother. "I promise I'll behave from now on," she vowed in a mocking tone.

"You're damn right, you will," Zack grumbled, beginning to give in, as he always did. "And I'm staying right here with you to make sure that you do behave." A conciliatory smile tugged at his lips.

Even though she refused to let it show, Kit was relieved at Zack's dictate; in truth, she welcomed his protection. She'd have welcomed Logan's, as well. Still avoiding his eyes, she smiled pertly at Zack.

"I'll be eighteen at the end of this month. I suppose I can put up with your overbearing attitude until then."

Shaking his head, Zack grinned at Logan. "What are we going to do with this spoiled brat?" he moaned in feigned exasperation.

"It appears you're going to baby-sit," Logan retorted in an aloof tone. "I've got more important things to do."

Though Kit started with hurt surprise, she managed to keep her lips tightly together. Zack asked the question burning her tongue.

"You're leaving?"

Logan nodded sharply. "Tomorrow morning." A cynical smile twisted his lips. "You heard the *lady*. By the end of the month you'll be redundant. *I've* got a ranch to run." It was then that he glanced at Kit, his eyes remote. "In case I should miss the momentous occasion, happy birthday, *Miss* Aimsley."

Eight years removed from that scene, Kit could still feel the searing pain of Logan's abrupt departure, physically and emotionally. Though she had buried her feelings deep inside, the wound was once again a throbbing reality.

Weariness dragging at her, Kit returned to the bedroom and her now cold bed. Sleep was a tantalizing, illusive escape denied to her throughout the dark hours. The eerie half light of predawn was a ghostly specter on the landscape before she found surcease in the arms of Morpheus. Yet, even in slumber, the question that had caused the resurrection of the memory Kit had suppressed for so very long, rose to haunt her tired mind.

Had Logan's parting statement been a spur of the moment sally or a deliberately planned verbal dig?

Kit slept through the sound of her alarm and woke late and unrefreshed. Foregoing a cup of much needed coffee, she made do with a quickly gulped glass of juice. After a quick shower, she dressed swiftly but smartly in a charcoal-brown skirt suit that contrasted attractively with her pale skin and silver-sheened blond hair.

While applying a light, concealing makeup to her wan face, Kit felt grateful for the tricks taught her by various movie makeup artists she'd met during her years of film work. For, while she harbored no burning desire to become a "star," Kit had continued to audition for, and receive, major roles in more than a dozen films. She enjoyed the work, it paid well, and, as she had laughingly told her disgruntled father and brother, it kept her off the streets.

This particular morning, Kit's training in the film industry worked rewardingly to her advantage. By the time she turned away from her makeup mirror, not a trace of the ravages inflicted by her restless night remained on her face to betray her.

Mindful of Flint Falcon's promise to call her at her office that morning, Kit strode purposefully from her apartment. The phone inside the apartment began ringing as she pulled the door shut, snapping the lock into place. Listening to the trilling summons, Kit hesitated a moment, then, with a fatalistic shrug, turned away. She had forgotten the phone before she stepped into the elevator. She had more important things on her mind—such as the sale of the casino, and whether or not she should try out for a part in a film to be shot on location in Las Vegas, and exactly what the hell Logan had meant with his parting shot of the night before.

Kit worried the question all the way to the casino, at times positive she was blowing a casual remark way out of proportion, at others just as positive he had meant the remark as a verbal slap.

Kit had worked herself into a simmering anger by the time she parked her car at the casino. Now convinced that Logan was once again playing the heavy-handed big brother, and not in the least interested in getting to know the woman she'd become, Kit strode into her office prepared for war.

But this time, Kit vowed silently, flinging her body into the desk chair, it would be a war between the sexes, not between brother and sister.

Damn you, Logan McKittrick! Kit gritted her teeth and glared at the wall. Why hadn't he simply administered lecture number four and let it go at that!

Five

Controlled violence revealed by the raised tendons on his wrist and the white-knuckled grip of his fingers, Logan carefully replaced the receiver on the cradle of the stark black phone.

Damn it to hell!

Impatience drew his lips into a thin, tight line.

Of all the ill-timed, inopportune...! Frustration scored grooves on his face and tautened the long muscles in his thighs. Swinging away from the phone, Logan strode to the wide glass doors that led onto a balcony patio.

Why now? He groaned, raking stiff fingers through the sleep-ruffled strands of auburn hair curling slightly at the back of his neck. Why had his cousin picked this particular time to come to him for moral support? A grimace twisting his lips, Logan replayed the telephone conversation in his mind.

"I'm here, at the ranch, Logan," Leslie had said without preamble. "I need to talk to somebody sane."

"What's the problem, honey?" Though Logan scowled, his response was gentle; Logan genuinely liked his cousin. Leslie Fairfield was the only child of Logan's father's sister and all her life, Leslie had turned to Logan in times of trouble.

"I'm in the throes of a messy divorce."

"I'm sorry to hear that, Leslie." Logan's sentiment was sincere—as far as it went. He *was* sorry if she was suffering, but he wasn't surprised at the outcome of her marriage. Secretly, Logan had doomed the alliance to failure from the outset.

"Logan, could you possibly come home?" Leslie wasn't quite successful at hiding the tremble in her voice. "If I don't talk to someone soon, someone who really cares, I'm afraid I'm going to start tearing at my hair."

"You'd damn well better keep your hands away from that gorgeous mane!" Logan ordered. "I have some business I must take care of, but I'll be home as soon as I can," he'd promised.

Staring sightlessly at the bright fall morning, Logan sighed heavily. What else could he have possibly said to Leslie? He certainly couldn't have confided to her that he was having problems with his own love life. Hell, he thought wearily, at this point, he didn't even know if he *had* a love life!

Kathryn.

Kit.

His Kit.

Damn!

He'd have to call her, explain about Leslie.... Logan shot a glance at the phone. Had Kit arrived at her office yet? Since he'd tried to reach Kit minutes before Leslie's call, Logan knew Kit was not at the apartment. Pivoting, he headed back to the black instrument.

Kit was still glaring at the wall when Mike entered her office. Annoyed at his unannounced entrance, she transferred her quelling stare to him.

"Have you ever heard of knocking?" she asked icily.

"I do humbly beg your pardon!" Mike exclaimed softly in surprise—Kit had told him repeatedly that it was unnecessary for him to knock.

"I'm sorry." Kit lowered her lashes over her anger-bright eyes. Why was she taking her frustration out on Mike? she berated herself. A conciliatory smile curved her lips as she looked up at him. "I'm not in the best of moods this morning."

Mike shrugged away her apology. "We all have our days." Returning her smile, he approached the desk, a small slip of paper in one hand. "He called three times, the last less than ten minutes ago—" handing her the piece of paper, he stepped back "—apparently while you were on your way in here."

"Thank you." Kit skimmed the message written on the paper in Mike's neat, bold script. The phone calls had been from Logan. The message was brief and terse.

Hold Falcon off. I'm needed at the ranch—will contact you later this afternoon.

A frown marred the perfection of Kit's carefully applied makeup as she raised her gaze from the paper to Mike.

"That's all Logan said?"

"That's it." Mike nodded, then added, "except that he'd tried to reach you at home first."

"Okay, thanks Mike." Kit sighed. "Were there any other calls?"

"Nope." Mike grinned as he sauntered to the door. "It's been a slow morning."

Kit went back to staring at the wall when the door shut on Mike. She also went back to a state of simmering anger. Although the mystery of who'd been ringing her phone as she left the apartment was now solved, Kit was fuming about Logan's abrupt departure.

What was so all-fired important at the ranch that Logan had taken off like a rocket, not even waiting long enough to talk to her personally? Kit's eyes narrowed suspiciously as she contemplated the question. The answer she came up with tinged her pale cheeks the color of outraged embarrassment.

Damn the man! Pushing her chair away from the desk, Kit jumped to her feet to pace the floor like a criminal on death row. The doubt she'd clung to concerning Logan's motivation the night before burned to ash in the flame of her fury. Kit was now certain that Logan's act of contrition and plea for better understanding between them had been no more than a new variation on the old theme of "teach little Kit a lesson in the proper and circumspect behavior of a well-brought-up young lady."

Damn him!

Kit had to grit her teeth to keep herself from shouting the curse aloud. If she hadn't been expecting a call from Mr. Falcon, she would have followed Logan to the ranch and taken a strip off his blasted hide!

Her slender body stiff with indignation, her emotions raw with disappointment, Kit fought the release of tears by forcing herself to attend to the business of the casino. Systematically sorting through the mail that had accumulated during the weeks she'd been in California, she managed to keep herself from glancing at the clock, while willing the phone to ring.

Had Logan arrived at the ranch yet? The question played havoc with Kit's concentration as she perused the information contained on a young woman's application for a job as a drinks waitress at the casino. The phone finally rang as Kit was making a note to set up an interview with the applicant. Snatching up the receiver, she answered breathlessly.

"The Silver Lining."

"Good morning, Ms. Aimsley." Disappointingly, it was Flint Falcon's quiet voice that came over the wire. "I apologize for not calling at the arranged time. I was tied up with a business call from my home in New Mexico."

Kit grimaced at the phone—was there an epidemic of "calls from home" going around? "An apology isn't necessary, Mr. Falcon. I was working and didn't even notice the time." *Liar,* she accused herself silently. "And since I haven't been able to set up a meeting between you and Mr. McKittrick, I'm afraid I'm the one who needs to apologize."

"Not at all," Falcon returned smoothly. "As a matter of fact, I'm relieved to hear that you were not successful."

Kit's hopes for a sale dropped like a lead weight. "You no longer want to buy the Silver Lining?" she said, her tone reflecting her disappointment.

"On the contrary. I want to buy the casino now more than ever," he corrected, a hint of exaltation coloring his usually controlled voice. "But I must return to New Mexico for a week or so and, since Mr. McKittrick has thus far resisted meeting with me, I didn't want to annoy him by canceling, in the event that you had arranged a meeting, that is."

"I see." Kit's hopes rose again.

"Did he flatly refuse to meet with me?" Falcon asked.

"Oh, no," Kit hastened to assure him. "Logan agreed to a meeting, but business called him back to his ranch this morning. He requested I put the appointment with you on hold." Kit's teeth were close to grinding by the time she finished speaking.

"Good." There was almost a purr to Falcon's tone. "Then suppose I call you when I get back to Tahoe," he suggested.

"All right, Mr. Falcon," Kit agreed. "By then, hopefully, I'll have a definite appointment for you."

Kit was even more agitated after Flint Falcon's call than she had been earlier. Unable to settle back to work, she paced the small office, muttering imprecations at the absent Logan McKittrick. To Kit's way of thinking, Logan's use of the pretext that he was needed at the ranch was wearing very thin.

How many times had he used the ranch as an excuse to avoid facing her? Kit's eyes narrowed as she contemplated Logan's overworn ruse. As far as she was concerned, Logan had been offering the plea of pressing business at the ranch as a convenient escape hatch...an escape hatch from *her*!

Kit paused in her pacing to rake her long, pearly-tinted fingernails through her hair. A deep sigh disturbed the quiet in the small room. Until the night of her graduation party, Logan had often taken her with him to the ranch when his presence was required.

Coming to an abrupt halt, Kit stared reproachfully at the phone on her desk. It had been years since Logan had spontaneously invited her to the ranch—exactly eight years.

Logan's habit of retreating to his ranch had begun the day after her graduation party. And, even then, he hadn't even bothered to offer the excuse personally. Kit had received the information secondhand through Zack. Logan had fallen back on the excuse again several months after her party, the day following his grim-lipped rescue of her in the alps. Throughout the long years since Kit's ignominious rescue from Drake's lecherous intentions, Logan had spent longer and longer periods of time at the ranch.

Trying to establish a pattern, Kit mentally scrutinized Logan's periods of retreat. Surprisingly, she found she could mark them like milestones along the road to her maturity.

There was that Fourth of July family gathering the year after her graduation from high school. Kit had invited a date to the family celebration, a young assistant director from the film company she was working with at the time. Logan had taken an immediate dislike to Tim, or Tom, or whatever his name had been. Claiming business, Logan had departed for Nevada on July fifth.

Then there was that debacle at Christmas four years ago...the one and only time Kit had seriously considered marrying another man. The man was Kevin Dawn, the brother of Kit's closest friend, Riana Dawn. Kit had mentioned the possibility of her accepting Kevin's proposal when her family, Logan included, had convened around the heavily laden table for Christmas dinner. Logan, Kit recalled, had eaten little, and had disappeared from California days before New Year's Eve and the party that Kit had considered the perfect time to announce her engagement. And so, he was no longer on the scene when Kit gently but firmly refused Kevin's marriage offer.

There had been several instances since that fateful Christmas dinnertime when Logan had simply, silently, removed himself from Kit's vicinity. The last time was merely a few weeks ago when she'd attempted to pin him down about selling the Silver Lining.

And now Logan had again made good his escape.... Kit felt positive that this time his flight was due to their conversation the night before. He'd made his point very effectively—what more was there to say?

"Plenty!"

Kit snapped the decision aloud as she strode to the door. This time Logan McKittrick had gone too far! How dare he suggest they get to know each other as man and woman instead of brother and sister, then take off for the ranch, leaving her with only a phone message?

Well, this time Logan was going to have company in his ready-made escape hatch! Kit decided, her step firm as she went in search of Mike Harmon.

The rattle of slot machines and the excited voices of people clustered around gaming tables washed over Kit as she entered the casino.

"Dealer pays eighteen."

Kit caught the quiet voice of a blackjack dealer as she passed one of the curved tables.

"Yo!"

A smile quirked the corners of Kit's lips at the sound of exuberance in a man's voice as she skirted the craps table—the delighted player had tossed the dice for an eleven.

"Ohmigosh, three plums!"

Kit slanted a glance at the young woman standing at a quarter machine that was clattering out the win of fourteen coins into the narrow tray attached to the machine.

"Looking for me?" Mike asked dryly at her shoulder.

"Oh!" Startled, Kit spun around to face him. "Yes, as a matter of fact I was."

"Well, you've found me. What can I do for you?"

"Hold down the fort again for a while?" Kit asked, coaxingly, giving him her very best smile.

"Of course." Mike smiled back.

Some of the tension eased out of Kit. "Thanks, Mike," she murmured, turning back to her office to retrieve her purse. She took a few steps, then shot a grin at him over her shoulder. "Remind me to give you a raise."

Cradling his cousin in a protective embrace, Logan carefully angled his arm to get a glimpse of the thin gold watch circling his wrist. A groan vibrated in his throat as he noted the late hour.

What must Kit—Kathryn, he automatically corrected himself—*be thinking by now?*

Not wanting to speculate on the possible virulent nature of Kit's thoughts, Logan stroked his cousin's back soothingly. The caressing action stirred memories of the night before, of his hands stroking Kit's slender back.

Lord, holding Kit in his arms was heaven. Being away from her was hell.

But what else could he have done? Logan swallowed a sigh and continued to soothe the tremors from Leslie's shaking body. Leslie had come to him for help, as she'd always come to him when she needed moral, and at times financial, support. He'd always been there for her. Logan couldn't conceive of refusing Leslie now, when she was going through the most traumatic experience of her life.

Kit and Leslie. Leslie and Kit. A faint smile lightened Logan's bleak expression. With no siblings of his own, Logan had first adopted his tiny, titian-haired cousin when he was five and she was three. Then he'd added to his "family" when Kit was born, seven years later. Throughout the girls' growing-up years, Logan had regarded both Kit and Leslie equally, with affectionate protectiveness. It was when Kit began to mature, at least physically, that his feelings had altered dramatically, uncomfortably.

Toward Leslie, Logan would always remain the supportive older brother. But toward Kit . . . Kit . . .

A noise, almost indiscernible, intruded on Logan's introspection.

It was dark before Kit arrived at the ranch. Driving carefully, she finally negotiated the private road leading to the ranch house. Except for a light from the room Logan used as a combination office-study, the house was in darkness.

Feeling nervous now that she was within striking distance of her quarry, Kit approached Logan's home with trepidation. The rustic beauty of the house was shrouded by the overcast night and the structure seemed to loom menacingly before her.

Shrugging off the sudden sensation that she was making a big mistake, Kit mounted the three steps to the wide porch that fronted the entire width of the building. Acting out of habit, she crossed the porch and reached for the doorknob; Kit couldn't remember a time when she'd ever knocked on the wide ranch-house door.

The spacious foyer was dark, as was the large living room to the right of it. Turning to her left, Kit walked unerringly along the open railed hallway that led to Logan's bedroom, private bath, and office-study. With every step Kit grew steadily more apprehensive.

Was Logan sleeping? she wondered anxiously. Had he retired for the night and left the light burning in his office? Kit knew from past experience that Hattie, Logan's housekeeper for twenty-odd years, sought her bed soon after the supper dishes had been cleared away and her kitchen restored to pristine order. Being an individual who needed at least eight or nine hours' sleep in order to function properly, Hattie was usually in bed before nine, as she was always up before four a.m.

Beginning to feel uncomfortably like a thief in the night, Kit paused at the closed door to Logan's office. Suddenly warm in her suede jacket, she shrugged out of it and draped it over her arm, her gaze fastened onto the thin line of light visible on the floor beneath the door.

What to do? Indecision pulled Kit in opposite directions. Part of her urged for a show of boldness by grasping the knob and entering the room. The other part pressed for cautionary action in the form of retreat.

Kit teetered uncertainly between the tug-of-war, then reached out to curl her trembling fingers around the knob.

Caution be damned! she thought bracingly, pushing the door open.

The door hinges were as scrupulously maintained as all of Logan's other possessions; the door opened without a whisper of sound. Moving forward, Kit entered the dimly lit room, her tread silenced by the deep pile of the wall-to-wall carpet. The scene that met her startled eyes stopped Kit three steps into the room.

Logan was in the room, but so was someone else…a woman. Kit's view was partially blocked by the back of the sofa that the couple were seated on, but she could see the firelight from the huge stone fireplace glinting off his auburn hair. Seated against the arm of the sofa, his head was lowered protectively over the woman held in his arms. The woman's back was to Kit, her face buried in the curve of Logan's broad shoulder. All Kit could see of her was the upper part of her slender body, the back of her head, and the flaming mass of her red hair.

Every muscle in Kit's body went slack as a crushing sense of defeat washed over her. The jacket slid down her arm, then to the floor unnoticed. There was an odd feeling of numbness, a numbness Kit feared would be short-lived. Within those desensitized seconds visions flashed into her mind, robbing the brightness from her blue eyes.

The visions were of an incident from six months before, of the night Kit had run into Logan in a restaurant in San Francisco. Kit had driven into the bay city for the weekend to attend a showing of the works of several promising young sculptors, one of whom was her closest friend.

Flushed with the success of the previous night's showing, the young sculptor had insisted Kit accompany her to the well-known, shockingly expensive restaurant.

Laughing and chattering together as they'd done since their school days, Kit and her friend had swept into the restaurant, and come face to face with Logan in the establishment's elegantly decorated foyer. Logan had not been alone. The woman who'd been clinging to his arm like a creeping vine was breathtakingly beautiful and possessed the most fantastic mane of red hair Kit had ever seen. As Logan introduced Kit and her friend to his companion, an exchanged look of intimacy between the couple told their story more eloquently than mere words. Kit knew instinctively that Logan and the redhead were lovers.

But that had been six months ago. Kit had believed that Logan's affair with the woman had ended long since.

Wishful thinking. Kit bit her lip to contain a cry of protest against her thoughts. *Obviously the affair has been ongoing. The redhead was the reason for Logan's hasty return to the ranch. What now of his plea for better understanding between them?*

The sudden sharp pain was unbelievable in its intensity. Kit's moment of numbness was over. Afraid she'd scream in agony from the searing pain squeezing the breath from her chest, the life from her heart, Kit shut her eyes tightly to blot out the scene, and took one careful step back. The quiet sound of Logan's voice halted her retreat.

"Stay where you are."

The woman stirred. Hating her, loving him, Kit shifted her anguished glance from one to the other, shaking her head as if to deny the truth.

Run! The order exploded in her mind. As Kit's body jerked to obey, Logan repeated his command in a harsh tone.

"Stay where you are!"

The woman moved away from him, and Logan slowly got to his feet. His hard-eyed stared kept Kit immobile. He murmured something that Kit felt positive was an apology, then walked around the sofa toward her.

"Why are you here?" he asked, frowning. "Is something wrong?"

Something wrong! Kit bit back a burst of hysterical laughter. *Everything* was wrong.

"No." Stepping back, Kit shook her head.

Logan's frown darkened. "Kit, you look strange." His stride swiftly closed the distance between them. "What is it? What's the matter?"

Did having the sickening sensation of bleeding to death inside make one look strange? Kit wondered wildly, retreating before his determined advance.

"Are you sick?" Logan's voice was sharp with concern.

Sick from love with you. Sick with my own foolish hopes and childish dreams, Kit told him mutely, as again she shook her head in denial.

"No, I'm not sick." She wet her dry lips. "I—I wanted to discuss something with you." She raked her mind for a reason for her unannounced visit, and blurted the first thought that came into her head. "I, ah, wanted to talk to you about my conversation with Flint Falcon."

"You drove out here to the ranch for that?" Skepticism edged Logan's soft voice. "Kit, what's going on?" he demanded.

Kit. She moaned silently. *What happened to Kathryn, and all the talk of getting to know each other?* But Kit couldn't ask him, wouldn't put her pain into words. She took another step back.

"Nothing's going on," she insisted. "I didn't mean to intrude." She slid her foot back another half step. "I'll talk to you tomorrow—or sometime."

"Damn it, Kit!" Logan growled, stepping to her and clasping her arms. "You're not—"

"If you will excuse me, I'll go to my room."

Kit's glance flew to the source of the soft, husky voice. The redhead had come up to Logan's side. Her eyes were swollen from weeping, her fair skin was blotchy, and though it had been some years since Kit had seen her, she recognized Logan's cousin at once.

"Leslie?" Instant relief rushed through Kit, only to be followed by a sense of confused consternation.

"Yes." The older woman nodded. "Leslie, the troublesome cousin." An apologetic smile shadowed her pale lips. "Hello, Kit. I'm sorry I can't stay and talk to you, but I feel about ready to drop." Rising on her toes, she kissed Logan's cheek before moving away from him. "Good night." As she passed Kit she smiled again and touched her lightly on the arm below Logan's hand. "You don't realize your own strength, Logan. Don't hurt her." Leslie walked from the room as she cautioned her cousin.

Though Logan's grip eased, he didn't release her. "Was I hurting you?" he asked softly, worriedly.

"No." Kit shook her head distractedly. What was going on? Surely Logan and Leslie hadn't had an argument? Logan and Leslie *never* argued, at least not seriously. Curious, yet hesitant about asking, Kit merely stared at him.

"Why are you looking at me like that?" Logan asked.

"Like what?"

"Like you'd just witnessed me committing a crime or something." His eyes narrowed. "What are you thinking? I made Leslie cry?"

"Did you?" Kit countered.

"Of course not!" Logan snapped. Then, sighing deeply in exasperation, he spun around and drew her to the sofa.

"Is Leslie the reason you had to rush back here this morning?"

"Yes." Lifting a hand, Logan raked his fingers through his already disheveled hair. "Sit down, Kit, and I'll explain."

"But you don't owe me an—" she began in protest.

"Sit down, Kit!" Logan cut her off roughly.

Kit sat. Her body rigid, she glared at him defiantly as he lowered his big frame next to her.

"I *do* owe you an explanation," he sighed, resting his head against the sofa's high back. "I left a message that I'd call, and I didn't. I'm sorry."

"Why didn't you call, Logan?"

Logan turned his head to give her a dry smile. "Because I was kept too damn busy trying to convince Leslie that she was still an attractive woman."

Kit wasn't at all sure she liked the sound of his explanation. Exactly how, she mused uneasily, had Logan gone about convincing Leslie? Uncomfortable with her speculations, Kit lowered her eyes. Logan read her expression like an open book.

"Oh, for heaven's sake!" he gritted impatiently. "I didn't convince her the obvious way, if that's what's freezing you!"

Kit felt her face flush with color. "Why was she feeling unattractive in the first place, Logan?" she asked contritely.

"Because that bastard she married made her believe it." Fury vibrated on his voice.

"But why?" Kit exclaimed.

"The obvious reason," he said tiredly. "He wanted to play around and needed an excuse. She's divorcing him, but she's devastated."

"And, of course, she came to you." Kit smiled. "As both your *little* sisters do when they need comfort."

"It's been a long time since you've come to me for comfort." Bringing his hand up, he stroked her cheek with the back of his fingers. "Then again, as I indicated last night, I no longer think of you as my little sister."

Kit suddenly had trouble breathing. "How do you think of me?"

Moving lazily, Logan shifted closer to her. "In ways that would probably shock you out of your mind," he murmured as he brought his head to hers and brushed his lips over her mouth.

Six

_____

It certainly is warm in the room. Must be the heat from the fire. Flustered, oddly excited and a little frightened all at the same time, Kit's thoughts fragmented as Logan's lips brushed hers again. With a flutter, her eyelashes began to lower. Her mind drifted to stun.

"Honey?"

Rousing herself with an effort, Kit focused on Logan's frowning face. "Hmm?" she murmured in answer.

"Why were you looking at me so strangely when you came in?"

Kit was suddenly much warmer, especially from the neck up. She also found it difficult to meet Logan's steady gaze.

"Kathryn, tell me."

On the point of dissembling, or even lying out-right, Kit bit her lip in chagrin at his use of her proper name. Logan was not speaking to a child, he was speaking to a woman—and expecting an honest answer. Sighing, Kit accepted the fact that he had very neatly boxed her in to telling the truth.

"I thought she was someone else," she said, all in a rush, very softly.

Logan blinked. "Would you mind running that by me again? I think I missed something."

"I said, I thought Leslie was someone else when I first came in," Kit said distinctly.

"But who?" Logan persisted, clearly baffled.

Glancing down, Kit watched as her fingers laced together. "That woman you introduced me to in San Francisco last summer." Her voice went low. "That redheaded woman—I don't remember her name."

"Her name was Doreen." Blatant male amusement accented Logan's tone. "And I don't believe you."

Kit's head jerked up. "I don't remember her name!" she exclaimed indignantly.

"Not that." Logan's lips twitched. "I meant that I can't believe you thought Leslie was Doreen. They look nothing alike."

"I only saw the back of Leslie's head, and her hair is very similar to that woman's!"

"Doreen," Logan said chidingly.

"All right! Dor-een." Kit drew the name out bitingly.

"A lovely woman." Logan's purring tone was accompanied by a smile.

That lovely woman looked like she was for sale to the highest bidder! Kit retorted silently. "Yes," she agreed reluctantly. "Um, how is...Doreen?" she probed softly.

"Damned if I know." Logan moved his head against the sofa. "But I suspect she's just fine." His lips curved sardonically. "Doreen is definitely a survivor."

"You don't, ah, see her any more?"

Logan's amusement erupted into soft laughter. With the tip of one finger, he outlined her lips.

"No, I don't, ah, see her anymore. I haven't seen her, in fact, since that night in San Francisco." His laughter faded as his tone grew jagged. "What about you? Are you *seeing* anyone presently?"

Kit's lips tingled in response to his teasing touch. Her breathing was decidedly erratic. A dozen questions crowded into her head as he spoke—questions like: why aren't you seeing her any more? And, why haven't you seen her since that night? And... All the queries were sent flying by his final word. *Presently?* Kit repeated the word to herself. A frown drew her pale brows together. Presently presupposed she had been seeing someone, or several someones, right along. Kit frowned in earnest. Did Logan believe her to be promiscuous? Horrified at the very idea, Kit caught her lip between her teeth...and nearly caught Logan's finger in the bargain.

"Hey, honey, you don't owe me an answer!" Logan's frown mirrored hers. "I didn't mean to stir up unhappy feelings. I know I have no right to pry into your love life."

What love life? Kit bit harder on her lip to contain the question trembling on her tongue. At the same time she was hard-pressed to keep the laughter from escaping her throat. Love life indeed!

"Ah, no, Logan, I'm not *seeing* anyone presently," Kit mumbled in a choked tone.

Intent on her own inner turmoil, Kit hadn't been aware of the tension in Logan until it visibly eased from him in a deep, soundless sigh.

"That's good," he murmured, resuming the play of his fingertip along her lower lip. "I was counting on your undivided attention."

Kit's mouth felt like a dried sponge. "Undivided attention?" she repeated—stupidly, she felt sure. "For...what?"

Logan's smile ignited tiny fires in every pulse point in her body. Fascinated, she watched his eyes darken to emerald. "For...whatever," he whispered, replacing his finger with his lips.

There was no teasing brush of his mouth against hers this time. For a man his size, Logan moved against her with the smooth agility of an athlete. His chest crushed her breasts at the same instant his lips took command of hers. His kiss was as hard as it was brief. A murmur of protest sighed through her lips when he drew away.

"Are you a woman now, little Kit?" His warm breath caressed her flushed face.

Thrown into confusion, Kit blinked and stared into the gemlike glitter in his eyes. What was he getting at? she wondered, struggling out of the sensuous fog clouding her mind.

"Yes." For all her breathlessness, Kit's voice was strong with conviction.

"I was hoping you'd say that." Logan's final word was whispered against her mouth. "Part your lips for me, Kathryn. Invite me in." His teeth nipped delicately at her lower lip as an added inducement.

If he had expected an argument, Logan received a pleasant surprise. Eagerly, hungrily, Kit opened her mouth as she raised her head the fraction needed to mold her lips to his. The result of her action was instant combustion, a conflagration that spontaneously flashed out of control, sweeping away all thought, all inhibition.

Logan accepted her silent offer eagerly and hungrily. A low growl vibrating his throat, he slipped his tongue into the moist interior of her mouth.

"Sweet, so sweet."

Kit felt, more than heard, his murmur of appreciation. Responding to the tremor, the tone of his voice, she grasped his face between her hands, thrilling to the rasp of rough growth of beard along his jawline. Her move was incendiary. Logan's firm tongue thrust, filling her mouth, swamping her senses.

Closer; she had to get closer. The thought was unformed, yet clear. Sliding her hands back, Kit speared her fingers into the springy silkiness of his hair, tugging, urging an even deeper intimacy.

"God!" Logan expelled the exclamation harshly as he pulled away from her.

"Logan?" Afraid she'd been too aggressive, Kit looked at him fearfully, shivering from the expression of strain tautening his features. "What is it? What have I done?" she asked, her eyes widening with the first sting of tears.

Moving with a swiftness that made him a blur for an instant, Logan swept her up, only to immediately lay her down lengthwise on the long sofa.

"You've set me on fire, woman," he muttered huskily, aligning his body to hers. "And I think you might be in danger of burning in the blaze," he murmured at her ear a moment before gently sinking his teeth into her lobe.

Kit felt the reaction all the way to her toenails. Distractedly, she determined that burning up in his blaze was to be wished for devoutly. Hadn't she wanted this, to know him in just this way, for years? she mused absently, shuddering to the feel of his tongue gliding down her neck to the curve of her shoulder.

Oh, Logan, don't stop! Beyond speech, the plea echoed inside Kit's head. Suddenly terrified he'd withdraw, removing the warmth infusing her entire body with sensual life, Kit clung to him, arching her soft curves into the angular hardness of his aroused body.

"Yes, oh, yes!" Logan's voice was ragged with the need searing his body, making demands he was still in control of—marginally. One broad hand took possession of one delicately formed breast, fingers stroking, wrenching a gasp of pleasure from Kit's arched throat. Her gasp turned to a pitiful moan when his hand was removed.

"I must see you." Logan's voice was very low, harsh with desire. "I must touch you." His fingers were tugging at her clothes even as he spoke.

Years of experience were revealed by the smooth expertise of his hands as he swiftly divested Kit of every stitch of protective covering. Murmuring words of praise for her beauty, words that sent wave after wave of delight rushing to her head, he swept her garments from her, tossing them carelessly to the floor.

"You have the most beautiful legs I've ever seen on a woman."

Forcing her heavy lids up, Kit stared into the awed expression Logan made no attempt to conceal. Scorched by the heat blazing from his eyes, she quivered as his hand stroked the length of one of her legs, and whimpered sensuously as he tested the softness of her inner thigh. His palm was warm and excitingly rough against her silky skin. Kit's knee flexed, and tilted outward, invitingly. The ache deep inside her body expanded at the sound of the groan that was torn from Logan's throat.

"It's been so long." In one fluid motion he was on his feet, fingers working at the buttons on his shirt. His heated gaze held her still, shivering with anticipation. "So very long."

The hurt was blunt, not sharp enough to completely pierce the grip of sensuality, but strong enough to bring a question to her fuzzy brain. *Had Logan not been with a woman at all since Doreen?* Kit deflected the hurt instinctively. *Does it matter? Yes, of course it matters.* She shivered for a different reason. But, for now, she'd take what she could of him. Whatever he was willing to share of himself with her. Kit accepted the sense of hurt that accompanied the decision. She had no choice, not really. She'd also waited too long, wanted too long.

Logan's clothes were gone. He stood before her tall, proud, magnificent in his masculinity, his body taut, muscles quivering with need of her.

Kit's throat was too tight to allow the passage of words. Her eyes frankly adoring, she raised her arms to him in welcome.

With Kit's opened-arm gesture something shattered inside Logan. Ever since he'd kissed her, deeply, searchingly, the faint voice of his conscience had intruded, warning him against losing his head and forfeiting his control—something that had never happened to him, even as an overeager teenager.

Secure in the knowledge of his own strength, Logan had mentally brushed aside the cautioning voice. He would look at her, touch her, no more... but look and touch he must. He continued to feel confident in his strength of self as he'd eased the clothes from her slender body, and flung the garments from his own. And still he'd believed he was in absolute control.

And perhaps he actually was. Until Kit had arched her glorious body sinuously and held out her arms to him, perhaps Logan was still the man in control.

Eight years of need, and longing, and torment, and yes, even mind-searing guilt for all he was feeling for and about Kit, were pounded out of existence by the sight of her outstretched arms.

Like a man driven beyond the point of no return, Logan dropped to his knees on the carpet beside the sofa and scooped Kit into his arms. The need tearing at his body was torment, the feel of her satiny skin gliding along his was a promise of paradise.

Restraint dissolved by the accumulated passion rushing through his veins, Logan sank to the carpet, dragging Kit with him, beneath him.

Had Kit resisted by as much as a murmur of protest, it might have cleared the haze of desire compelling him toward the release gained by possession. Kit did not resist; Kit unconditionally surrendered.

Electrified by the brush of her soft thighs against the hair-roughened skin of his own, Logan gripped her hips, lifted her, and sought to be one with her with a single, piercing thrust.

He felt her cry of pain to the depths of his soul.

"No. No. No!" Logan's answering cry was clawed from the pain compressing his chest.

"Logan." Kit's soft tone offered comfort.

"No." Logan shook his head, refusing to believe the magnitude of his own stupidity. After all these years, years of jealousy eating at him like an acid while imagining her with another man, *several* other men, his sweet, adored Kit had been innocent, *innocent*! And *he* had approached her like a rutting boar! "Oh, God, no!"

"Logan, don't, please! I wanted it as much as you did!"

His face drawn with lines of agony, Logan closed his eyes. His body sheathed by hers, he slowly lowered his head to the pillow of her breasts.

"Forgive me, if you can. I can't forgive myself."

The tear that dropped to her breast burned Kit's skin like a naked flame.

"Logan!" Her eyes shimmering with tears, Kit stroked his hair, his cheeks, his wet eyes. For a moment she groped for a way to reach into him and ease the pain. Her own pain caused by his forceful possession was gone. As was the gnawing emptiness she'd known since the night of her graduation party. How to tell him? How could she phrase it? Kit searched her mind an instant, then a small smile eased the anguish shadowing her eyes.

At a time like this, who needed words?

Slowly, testingly, Kit moved her hips. Her smile deepened when Logan stopped breathing. Light as air, she drifted her fingertips down the length of his spine. Logan shuddered. Like a cat, she arched her back. Logan groaned, and covered her breast with his trembling hand.

"Kathryn?" Self-recrimination was in his tone, but there was also a hint of hope.

"Um?" Kit's palm stroked his narrow hip.

"Are you sure?" Even as he asked, Logan pressed his lips to the budding tip of her breast.

"Ahh," Kit sighed with pleasure, "yes, I'm sure." There was a stir, inside, a throbbing pulse. "Oh!" Kit gasped, then laughed. "Oh, goodness!"

"Do you like that?" Logan wasn't playing teasing games, he was demanding an honest answer.

"I could become addicted." Kit moaned as she felt the renewed leap of life inside her body.

"I could become addicted to this." Moving slightly, Logan brought the tip of her breast to aching arousal with the curling action of his tongue.

"Oh, yes! Oh, please, yes!" Luxuriating in sensuousness, Kit's body responded wildly, undulating beneath the pressing weight of his. Logan shifted his hips, cautiously, testingly, burying deep into the tight warmth of her. At the same time he took her into his mouth, drawing on her breast greedily.

"Logan!" This time Kit's cry rang sweetly in his ears, for this time the cry was one of exquisite pleasure.

Then time and place faded. In a realm known only to lovers, Kit lost all sense of self. There were no decisions to be made, only physical dictates to be followed. Obeying the sense of urgency blindly, she arched up, inviting more and yet more of him, needing the completion of two halves fused into one whole. And, as she strove for that ultimate harmony, Kit murmured encouragement to Logan.

Goaded by the soft, inciting sounds Kit was making, Logan fought to hang on to his shredding control for the second time within one hour. It was a losing battle—perhaps because it was a battle he really didn't want to win.

Even through the haze of desire, Logan knew instinctively that the moment of attrition and remorse would come. He knew it, and ignored it. Now, this instant, his entire being was blazing out of control, but not only with the need for physical satisfaction. Unadulterated male triumph flowed in equal measure with the passion searing his body. Kit was *his. His!*

He, Logan McKittrick, was the first man to know her as a woman!

The knowledge was potent. Intensely aroused, Logan drove himself, and Kit, to the very edge of consciousness.

His efforts were rewarded by the most shattering, most explosive release and completion he'd ever experienced, an experience doubly sweetened by the cascading shudders that shook Kit's slender body and the muted scream of ecstasy that was torn from her throat.

* * *

Logan was awakened by stiffening muscles protesting the cold. Disoriented, sleepily confused, he frowned. *His front was warm... and cushioned!* Awareness came in a rush. *Kit! He was still with Kit, covering Kit, joined to Kit!*

Delicious.

For an instant Logan drifted along with the urge to slip back into the contentment of sleep. He yawned widely, drawing in the musky woman scent of Kit, and rubbed his beard-stubbled cheek against her silky breast. His action brought full alertness.

Kit's skin was cold!

Damned fool! He berated himself harshly. *She gives you the gift of her innocence, and you give her a hard floor in a cold room to sleep on!*

Logan's back was still shivering, but his face was now hot, heated by chagrin, shame, and the inevitable remorse.

Moving in his more usual, decisive way, Logan eased his weight from her slight form. As he rose to his knees the cold air swirled around his naked body. The fire had died—in the grate if not his body. It was late, or early, somewhere around 3:00 a.m. he judged. His green eyes as bleak as a January ocean, Logan gazed down at the single most important person in the world to him.

Kit was sleeping peacefully, a hint of a smile tilting the corners of her lips. Her tangled, disarrayed hair gleamed like a silver coin in the glow of the moonbeams slanting into the room through two elongated windows.

When had he turned off the lamp? Logan dismissed the query as superfluous. *What difference did it make? The lamp was off. The fire was out. The room was cold. Kit was beautiful in slumber. And Logan McKittrick was a jackass.*

Heaving a silent sigh, Logan bent to carefully slide his arms under Kit's supine body, wincing as he realized how very chilled her skin was.

As an indictment, jackass was woefully inadequate.

Slowly, lovingly, Logan gathered Kit's limp body close to his chest, then, flexing the strong muscles in his legs, rose to his feet, his anxious gaze fastened to her sleep-softened face.

Other than a murmur as she turned to burrow into his warmth, Kit slept on. The tender smile that pulled at Logan's lips revealed the combining emotions of love and caring, and the pain of remorse that was tearing him to pieces inside.

Moving unerringly in the dark hallway, Logan walked slowly to his bedroom. Shoving the slightly ajar door all the way open, he adroitly avoided the edges and corners of the massive oak furniture on his way to the equally massive bed. Getting the spread and covers down without jostling Kit awake became a self-imposed test of skill, which he managed with only one low grunt. Pulling the covers up to her chin and concealing the naked beauty of her became a point of honor. Turning his back on the bed became a feat of endurance.

Logan was tired—emotionally, physically, psychologically—and ached to slip into the bed beside her. A wave of acceptance swept him as he pulled on cotton briefs and stepped into faded jeans, carefully closing the zipper over his hardening body.

He wanted her. In exactly the same way as before. Hard. Fast. No holds barred. Both giving abandonedly to each other while receiving greedily.

A fine film of sweat slicked his palms as Logan buttoned his soft work shirt. Kit had wanted him. There was no way he could be mistaken about that. But Kit had been innocent. Had she wanted him— *Logan*? Or had she simply wanted him—the man?

Logan rationalized that there was nothing wrong if either of his speculations about Kit's possible motivation proved correct. Kit was twenty-five years old— long past the age when most lost their innocence. Even as he stamped his feet with unnecessary force into scuffed boots, Logan scathingly told himself to grow up.

As he entered his study to collect Kit's and his own discarded clothing, Logan shook his head sharply. Nothing, nothing had the power to diminish what he and Kit had shared—at least not for him. But, the crux of the matter was Kit. How would Kit regard Logan in the harsh light of morning?

Frowning, Logan retraced his steps to the bedroom, tossed the armful of clothes onto a chair, then, after a lingering glance at the sleeping woman in his bed, grabbed his sheepskin jacket from the closet and stormed from the room.

You've got some heavy thinking to do, old son, he advised himself irritably, jamming his hands into the pockets of his jacket as he loped to the stable. *And some conscience searching, as well. Don't make the mistake of thinking that Kit is now yours for the ask-*

ing—even if you do want her so badly you can taste it in every living cell in your body.

Kit is definitely her own person. The decision is hers.

His mind seething with the conflict between desire and fairness, Logan saddled up the large roan that was dancing in anticipation of a run. Pulling himself up onto the back of his horse, Logan turned in the direction of his favorite thinking place—the pine-covered hills on the west border of his property.

It was not until after Logan had allowed the roan a flat-out run that he was able to get down to the business of his relationship—or lack of same—with Kit.

Fall was lying easy on the ground; even in the foothills the temperature was mild. Yet Logan knew the weather situation could change swiftly, with wind driving snow from the mountains to the grazing lands, bringing winter in a single furious sweep.

But for now, the autumn aroma of pine needles crushed beneath the roan's hooves was comforting to Logan. It was a spicy, familiar scent. Inhaling the tangy smell of home, Logan let the roan pick his way over the uneven terrain, as he carefully picked his way through his own jumbled mass of conflicting thoughts and emotions.

Proceed with caution.

The intrusive voice of Logan's conscience was back, stronger than before—more intense, more certain.

Caution be damned! Logan argued with himself. *It's been nothing but caution for over eight years. How long can a normal, healthy man follow the course of caution?*

How great is the prize?

With a wry smile, Logan conceded the point to his persistent conscience. But it rankled; it rankled badly. The prize indeed was great, the highest he hoped to attain. The prize was a lifetime with Kit. Kathryn, Logan automatically corrected himself.

Kathryn.

Kit.

His Kit.

Logan's sigh blended with the gentle breeze soughing through the shivering pine boughs.

Kit of the silver hair and laughing eyes and long, elegant dancer's legs. Kit of the impulsive nature and fierce loyalties and slim, enticing body. Kit of the avid California beachboys and stance of independence and hot, sensual mouth.

And it was there, full-blown, in living color. Every instant of the scene was there, filling his mind, consuming his senses, making him sweat.

His breathing ragged, Logan slumped in the saddle. He could *see* her, *feel* her, *taste* her. The night before was now—right now. His body ached with an unrelenting need to look at Kit, touch Kit, be one with Kit.

Without conscious thought, Logan jerked on the reins, bringing the roan to an abrupt halt. Expertly trained by Logan, the animal stood docile, patiently awaiting the next command. It was a long time coming.

Staring into middle distance, Logan savored the exquisite torture his body was inflicting on him, and considered his less than precise mental condition.

He ached.

He needed.

He wanted.

But what about Kit?

Had their lovemaking drawn her closer to him, or had it set her free? Uneasy with the idea, Logan shook his head. Nevertheless, the thoughts continued to hammer at him, demanding his attention.

If the act of mutual physical possession had unlocked the door between youth and maturity for Kit, could he let her go?

The shaft of alarm that ripped through Logan was breathtaking in its intensity.

"No!" Logan didn't know or care that he cried the denial aloud.

Do you have the right to make that decision for her? Logan had the uncomfortable sensation that his conscience had actually sneered when it asked the question inside his head.

"No." This time Logan was fully aware of speaking, as fully aware as he was of exactly what he was admitting to.

He had taken the initiative, forced the issue. Just the day before, he had offered her friendship, an opportunity to get to know one another as equals. Then he'd reneged that offer by taking her innocence.

Because he loved her, could he now demand she love him in return?

No.

Seven

She was sore. Rolling over in the wide bed, Kit winced at the tug of pain in her thighs. Logan had not been gentle with her. Her lips curved wryly. Of course, Logan had reason to believe she was experienced. She'd worked at her facade of worldliness. If she was aching, she'd earned every pain.

A low burst of laughter smoothed Kit's lips into a grin. She had also earned for herself a wildly exciting initiation into womanhood!

A tingle slid down the length of Kit's spine. She had always known Logan was forceful—hadn't she witnessed the aggressive side of his nature countless times, in various situations? Kit's grin widened. This morning she could fully appreciate exactly how forceful Logan could be. The man was a veritable dynamo!

At the moment, the man was also among the missing. Without Logan's considerable bulk, the bed was extremely empty. Still fuzzy from sleep, Kit was not alarmed or hurt by Logan's retreat from her side. She had spent enough time at the ranch while she was growing up to know that Logan was an early riser, rarely sleeping beyond 5:00 a.m.

But, on second thought, Logan might have made an exception this morning. Kit frowned as the haze of sleep receded. *Where was he? Why wasn't he with her? After last night . . .*

Kit bit her lip. Just because what had happened between them last night was important to her did not necessarily mean it was all that important to Logan.

Logan hadn't been a virgin—not for a good long time. Making love with a woman would be as natural as breathing for a man as virile as Logan.

For a few seconds Kit allowed herself to feel insulted. Then her sense of fair play asserted itself. Logan had not taken one thing from her that she hadn't freely offered. What normal man would have refused?

With a sigh of resignation, Kit struggled to sit up, wincing again at the pull on the muscles of her inner thighs. What did she do now? Kit absently gazed about the room as she contemplated the question.

She had seen the room, Logan's room, many times before. Yet now, in the light of a new day, and her new status in his life, the room appeared subtly different.

From the no-nonsense weave in the drapes to the dark, clean lines of the heavy furniture, Logan's bedroom made a bold and definite statement of solitary masculinity. *Did the room reflect the man's prefer-*

ences? Kit didn't like the implication of the speculation, but she forced herself to acknowledge the conclusion her thoughts were leading her to.

Was Logan, by choice, a man alone?

Shoulders slumped, Kit stared sightlessly at the far wall. Logan was thirty-eight years old. And he certainly wasn't still in a single state for want of company. Kit grimaced. For years she'd personally viewed the hordes of females in *company* with Logan. No. Kit shook her head, underlining her decision. If Logan was unencumbered by wife or live-in lover, it was because Logan liked it that way.

So, where did that leave one lovesick Kathryn Aimsley? Kit mused unhappily. If she were honest, with him as well as herself, she would know her rights were few—as were her options.

Considering the kind of man that Logan was, Kit knew she could force the issue with him. His reaction to her virginal state gave her proof of that. If she requested marriage as payment for her innocence, Logan would marry her at once. Kit was as certain of his honor as she was of her love for him. But did she really want to be his wife badly enough to apply that type of pressure?

Yes! Kit's pulse leaped with the instantaneous thought.

No. Reason prevailed, if with a pout.

Suddenly restless, Kit scrambled from the bed. As she collected her clothes from the chair her course of action became clear in her mind. She had decided which option to pursue. She would lob the ball into Logan's court. The next play was his. And, even though patience had never been her strongest characteristic, Kit was determined to follow his lead in whatever direction he chose.

A hot shower eased most of the stiffness from Kit's legs. Carefully applied makeup gave her face a measure of serenity. The steam in the bathroom had removed the wrinkles from her clothes. As Kit walked out of the room she appeared as usual; the change on the inside didn't show.

Leslie sat hunched over a cup of coffee in the breakfast alcove. Her face looked ravaged in the unrelenting morning sunlight. She smiled encouragingly, if faintly, as Kit approached the round cherrywood table.

"Good morning." Leslie indicated a chair, then the glass coffeepot, with an absent wave of her hand. "The coffee's hot and there are warm muffins in the basket."

The aroma of blueberries wafted from the napkin-covered basket set in the center of the table. Murmuring a greeting, Kit slid onto a cherrywood chair. Feeling uncomfortable in the awkward silence that followed, Kit poured a cup of coffee for herself, plucked a muffin from the basket, then sat staring at both as if she'd never seen the like of either before.

"Logan's out somewhere."

Kit glanced up quickly at the diffident sound of Leslie's voice. Never had she heard Leslie sound other than supremely confident.

"Are you all right, Leslie?" Kit asked, noticing the grip the older woman had on the fragile-looking cup.

"No." Leslie gave a parody of a smile. "I feel like hell. But I'm not quite as bad as yesterday, and I'm beginning to have hopes for tomorrow."

Kit's throat tightened with compassion for the woman she'd admired throughout her growing-up years. Leslie had often been at the ranch during Kit's summer vacation visits, and she had never been other than kind to the self-admittedly volatile teenager Kit had been.

"Is there anything I can do?" Kit despaired at the inadequacy of her offer.

"Yes." Leslie surprised Kit with an immediate response. "You can talk to me for a while." The faint smile flickered on her pale lips again. "What is it about women that drives us to seek communion with our own kind whenever we are faced with an emotional crisis?"

Kit's smile reflected Leslie's. While showering, she had felt swamped by the need to talk to her mother.

"I think your answer lies in the phrase, 'Our own kind.' Only another woman can empathize emotionally." Kit sipped at her coffee, and broke her muffin into tiny pieces.

"Yeah." Leslie shrugged. "Logan tried, and his concern did help, but..." Her voice trailed away.

"But he got mad?" Kit asked on a flash of insight.

"Exactly." Leslie managed a brief but real smile. "He demanded to know why I was allowing the bastard to rip me apart like this."

"And wanted to know if he should go to New York and break the son-of-a-blank in half?" Kit guessed, accurately.

"Or even worse." Leslie laughed. "I think Logan mentioned something to the effect of relieving my ex of his skin, a layer at a time."

Kit controlled a grimace when she thought of Leslie's ex-husband, the heartthrob of the Broadway stage. For all his practised charm and handsomeness, Kit had never liked the actor Leslie had fallen in love with at first glance.

"You should have told him to go ahead," Kit said bluntly.

"I must admit I was tempted." For an instant the old familiar fire burned in Leslie's green eyes. Then she shrugged again. "What would it prove? It certainly wouldn't change anything."

"The marriage is definitely over?" Kit asked hesitantly.

"Definitely." Leslie's lips tightened. "You know what hurts most, Kit?" She raised her eyes to face Kit squarely. Kit shook her head. "Knowing he was sleeping around from the very beginning," she went on in a harsh tone. "He bragged to me about having a native woman while we were on our honeymoon in Martinique."

"That bastard!" Kit exclaimed. "I agree with Logan," she added heatedly. "That man's skin needs thinning!"

"Perhaps, but not by Logan." Kit smiled. "Speaking of Logan, how are you feeling about him this morning?"

All the indignation seeped out of Kit. "Uncertain," she admitted, suddenly looking very young.

Leslie smiled in understanding. "I can appreciate what you mean. One can never be sure of what Logan is thinking. He's a lot more complex than he appears on the surface."

And now, he's very likely feeling guilty, as well. Kit kept the thought locked in her mind. "I'm amazed he hasn't washed his hands of the two of us." She sighed. "Between us, we sure have given him enough grief."

"He loves us." Leslie reached across the table to lightly squeeze Kit's hand. "We're his family. And when Logan gives of himself, he gives completely. You know that... or at least you should."

"Yes." Kit's voice was little more than a whisper. "But now the situation has changed between me and Logan." She had to force herself to meet Leslie's calm stare.

"I know that, Kit." Leslie smiled at Kit's start of surprise. "Honey, I'm nearly ten years older than you. And I've been around a bit. I recognize the signs."

"Signs?" Kit repeated faintly.

"The subtle, telltale signs lovemaking leaves on a woman," Leslie clarified. Her eyes softened with the flush that tinged Kit's cheeks. "You love him, don't you?"

"I always have," Kit confessed.

"I mean, really love him," Leslie chided. "Not as a brother or friend, but as a man."

"I always have," Kit repeated, then qualified, "at least, ever since my teens." Feeling suddenly exposed, she glanced to the doorway into the kitchen. "Mrs. Randolf?" she asked, referring to the housekeeper.

"Don't worry, she's safely out of hearing range," Leslie assured. "She went outside to feed the chickens."

A sigh of relief whispered through Kit's lips. The last thing she needed was for Logan's housekeeper to overhear her. Staunchly loyal, and an incurable romantic, Mrs. Randolf would very likely try her hand at matchmaking.

"So—" Leslie lit a cigarette, her third since Kit entered the room "—how does Logan feel about you?"

This time Kit's sigh came straight from the heart. "I . . . don't know." She lifted her shoulders in a helpless gesture as Leslie raised her eyebrows in disbelief. "I know he has affection for me but, other than that, I simply don't know."

Leslie's smile was dry. "You could ask him, you know."

"Yes, I know, but . . ." Kit bit her lip.

"But?" Leslie prompted, crushing out the cigarette then immediately lighting up another.

Kit hesitated a moment, then blurted out, "I was a virgin, Leslie."

"Oh." Leslie's eyes widened in comprehension.

"Yes, oh." Kit laughed shakily. "You know Logan. If I told him how I felt, what do you think he'd do?"

"I don't even have to think about it, I know what he'd do." The older woman nodded in understanding. "Logan would insist on marriage—and die before he'd admit it wasn't what he wanted."

Having her opinion confirmed brought no joy to Kit. "I want him very badly, Leslie," she murmured. "But not badly enough to grab him at any cost. I won't shackle him to me if he doesn't wish to be shackled."

"I see what you mean. It would be agony for both of you." A cynical smile twisted her full lips. "Isn't life grand?"

"It should be."

Startled, both women glanced around. Seeming to fill the doorway, Logan stood propped against the door frame, his compassionate gaze resting on Leslie's haggard face.

"Did you get any sleep at all?" he asked gently, pushing away from the door and entering the room.

"Yes." Leslie met his disbelieving look directly. "I'm okay, Logan, really."

"Umm," he murmured noncommittally, switching his gaze to Kit. "And you, you slept well?"

Kit was unsuccessful in maintaining his stare. "Yes," she said softly, lowering her gaze to her empty cup. "I slept very well."

"Coffee's cold."

Kit glanced up quickly. Logan was holding the glass pot, a frown drawing his brows together. "Where's Hattie?"

"I'll make some." Kit pushed her chair back.

"I'm right here." Mrs. Randolf bustled into the room. "You just sit yourself right back down there, young lady," she said scoldingly to Kit. "I'll make fresh coffee while I'm getting breakfast." She swept their faces with a fierce glance as she plucked the pot from Logan's fingers. "Now, what'll you have? Eggs? Waffles? Corned-beef hash?"

"Hash," Logan replied at once. "With poached eggs."

"Just fresh coffee for me," Leslie said.

Positive she'd be unable to swallow a thing, Kit was about to second Leslie's request when Hattie Randolf planted her hands on her rounded hips. "Leslie, you need some food inside you. You look like a truck backed into you." She turned her determined glare on Kit. "That goes for you too, Kit. Now," she said firmly, "what'll it be?"

To Logan's obvious amusement, both women caved in to the grimly determined Hattie.

Kit did manage to eat a bit of the hash and part of the poached egg Hattie served minutes later. Not knowing what to say to Logan, she remained quiet throughout the meal. She tried to follow the conversation between Logan and Leslie, but her attention wandered until Logan pushed his plate away and reached for the coffeepot to refill all three cups.

"It's decided, then: you'll stay here for a while."

Shaken by his commanding tone, Kit flashed a glance at Logan, a sigh of relief escaping as she realized he was speaking to Leslie.

"If you insist," Leslie responded meekly, listlessly.

Suddenly Kit didn't feel meek or listless. She didn't feel up to a postmortem of the events of the night before, either. What she felt was an overwhelming urge to run away and hide. Since entering the room, Logan's manner had hardly been that of a man in love— or even that of a lover. A wild streak of impatience goaded her, an impatience with playing a waiting game. Kit knew she had to get away from Logan or she'd completely disgrace herself by begging him to love her. She was sliding her chair back from the table when he turned his hooded green gaze on her.

"Going somewhere?" He regarded her with unnerving steadiness.

"I, ah, must get back to the casino."

"Falcon." Logan bit the name out. "That's right, you wanted to talk to me about him last night."

Feeling like a coward, Kit grasped at the excuse. "Yes. Have you given the matter any thought?"

Logan's smile hurt her in some indefinable way. "I've made a decision, Kit. You can tell your Mr. Falcon I've agreed to sell."

Kit was aware of the bright sunshine pouring into the room. She was aware of Leslie's confused but interested expression. But, most of all, she was too aware of the pain searing her entire body. Logan was willing to sell. After months of disregarding her pleas and arguments, he had suddenly agreed to relinquish his twenty-five percent of the casino. Kit clenched her fingers to prevent them from betraying the tremor shaking her slender body. Hurting badly, Kit accepted Logan's sudden capitulation as a rejection of herself.

If he had hoped to ease her down gently, Kit thought with spreading anguish, he had miscalculated. But she couldn't let him see, couldn't let him know, how deeply he had injured her.

"Well, finally!" Kit forced a wobbly laugh. "I was beginning to think I'd be stuck in that casino for the rest of my natural life." Rising quickly, she slid the chair under the table, then turned away, blinking furiously against the hot sting of tears in her eyes. "Mr. Falcon will be delighted. I—I can't wait to tell him."

"Kathryn."

Logan's tightly controlled voice halted Kit's escape as she reached the doorway. "Yes?" she asked without turning around.

"It's not necessary for you to go tearing back at once. Falcon will keep a day or two."

A day or two! Kit flinched. *No way!* she thought frantically. There was simply no way she could spend another minute, let alone another day, in his home. He probably wanted her to keep Leslie company. Kit raked her mind for an excuse to leave, *any* excuse, and blurted out the first thought that came to mind.

"It's not only Mr. Falcon," she said in a rush. "I've been offered a small role in a film to be shot in Las Vegas, and I've decided to accept it."

"Still playing with the Hollywood set, huh?"

Kit was too consumed by her own pain to notice the odd sound of despair in Logan's voice. She tossed her silvery hair back in a show of carelessness.

"Why not?" Composing her features, she turned to give him a brilliant smile. "I like the work. It pays well, and it's fun." Her smile faltered as she glanced at Leslie. "If you're feeling better in a week or two, why don't you come visit me on the set in Vegas?"

Her smile sad, Leslie shifted her gaze from Kit to Logan then back again to Kit. "I just might do that. Take care, Kit."

"I will." On impulse, Kit went to Leslie and gave her a brief hug. "He's not worth a moment of your unhappiness. Forget him, Les." Kit used the nickname she'd used as a child. "Get out and have some fun."

"Is *fun* the criterion of the good life?" Logan's tone held a definite sneer.

Kit felt his barb to the depths of her soul. Spine straight, chin high, she challenged him with a look. "Yes," she said decisively. "Simply because fun, or joy, is the reward for honest work." Spinning on her heel, Kit forced herself to walk slowly from the room.

Pausing long enough to collect her jacket and hand-bag, she left the house with the sinking sensation that it would be a cold day before she returned to the ranch she loved almost as much as the man who owned it.

Kit broke the speed limit several times on the drive back to her apartment. Luckily the highway patrol seemed to be busy elsewhere and she arrived in Tahoe tense but without a ticket for unsafe driving.

Kit had been gone for little more than twenty-four hours, yet the apartment seemed alien and unwelcoming. As she shut the door, she felt an aching need to crawl into the arms of one of her brothers and have a good cry. But, even if one of them were available, how could she possibly answer the questions that would naturally be asked?

Logan doesn't love me.

No. Kit shook her head as she pushed her tension-stiff body away from the door she leaned on. No, she couldn't say that to either of the blond giants she claimed as her own. Zack, the cool-headed sculptor that he was, would very likely advise her to set her sights a little lower, and on someone closer to her own age. And Thack, laid-back character that he was, would probably offer to educate Logan, nonvi-olently, of course.

A wry smile flitted over Kit's lips. Either way, she'd be no better off than she was at that minute. Dropping her purse and jacket onto a chair, she crossed to the telephone. Her first call was to her agent, to tell him she'd decided to accept the film role, small as it was. Her second call was to her own office in the casino.

"The Silver Lining." The voice was melodic and Kit had a flashing image of Mike's secretary.

"It's Kit Aimsley, Kim," Kit said pleasantly—it was impossible to be other than pleasant to the efficient, sweet-tempered young woman. "Is Mike around?"

"He's on the floor, Ms. Aimsley. I'll buzz him."

"Back so soon?" Mike said when he came to the phone.

"Yes." Kit smothered a sigh. "Is there anything there that needs my attention?"

"There's a man camped outside your office," Mike informed her in a dry tone.

A man? Kit frowned. Who the devil...? "Mr. Falcon?" she wondered aloud.

"No. I never saw this guy before." Mike chuckled. "Tough-looking dude. Says he won't talk to anybody but you. Claims he has a message for you. He's been waiting since before noon."

Kit grimaced as she ran a glance down the length of her body. She felt rumpled from the long drive and crumpled from the emotional upheaval. She needed a soothing bath. She'd make do with a reviving shower.

"Well, I'm afraid he'll have to wait a little longer," she said briskly. "I'll be there in an hour or so, Mike."

It was closer to an hour and a half when Kit pulled her car into her private slot on the parking lot at the casino. Revitalized by a shower and fresh clothing, she strode to the private entrance at the side of the building that gave direct access to the business offices.

A man rose from his chair as Kit walked into the small office manned by her secretary during the day. A shiver tingled the length of her spine at the sight of him.

Kit was uncomfortably aware of an immediate sense of intimidation, but it wasn't caused by the size of him. At about six feet, he wasn't nearly as tall as her brothers or even Logan, nor was he as broad. Yet every inch of his lean, rangy body appeared poised, ready for anything. He had dark skin and hair, and his facial features were roughly chiseled. And he stared with unnerving directness at Kit out of the most incredible sapphire-blue eyes she'd ever seen. After pausing for an instant on the threshold, Kit stepped into the room, her hand extended.

"I'm Kit Aimsley," she said calmly. "You wanted to see me?"

The blue eyes barely flickered and revealed nothing, yet Kit had the sensation of being weighed and measured—with exact accuracy.

"That's right, ma'am. I come to you with a note pinned to my coat." His eyes began to gleam from amusement at the look of astonishment on Kit's face. "At least figuratively."

Kit's surprise had as much to do with his deeply attractive voice as with his amazing statement. "A note?" Kit repeated blankly, unconscious of the fact that he still held her hand inside his.

"My name's Josh Barnet." He applied a light pressure on her hand, then released it. "Thack sent me."

"Thack!" Kit exclaimed, thoroughly confused. "But why?" But before he could respond, she said, "Isn't Thack in Palm Springs?"

"Yes, ma'am." A slow smile curved his lips. "As a matter of fact, I'm relieved you arrived when you did." He shot a quick glance at the plain stainless-steel watch on his wrist. "He'll be calling here shortly, to confirm my identification."

Completely lost, yet intrigued, Kit returned his smile as she headed for her office. "Well, then, won't you come in?" Swinging the door open, she ushered him inside. "You can explain while we wait." Passing her desk, she went to the liquor cabinet set against the far wall. "Will you have a drink, Mr. Barnet?" Kit didn't much care if he wanted one or not, she needed one.

"Thank you, yes. I'll have a beer, if you have it."

Kit slanted a sparkling glance at him. "This is a casino, Mr. Barnet. If there's no beer in here, I'm sure there's one to be found in the lounge."

"J.B."

Bending over, Kit removed a small bottle of beer, and a likesize bottle of white wine from the compact refrigerator. "I beg your pardon?" she asked, frowning as she handed him the beer.

"I said to call me J.B." Plucking the wine from her hand, J.B. opened it and poured the wine into a fluted glass he'd found on top of the cabinet. It was at that moment Kit noticed that he used his left arm awkwardly.

"Is your arm injured, Mr., ah, J.B.?" she asked as she watched him open the beer.

"My arm is artificial, Ms. Aimsley," he replied smoothly.

Kit's eyes widened with shock, but before she could say anything, or even think of anything *to* say, he was easing past the rough moment with his low, beguiling voice.

"Now don't go getting all flustered and sympathetic on me. It happened some time ago. I've accepted it.'' He flashed a grin that dazzled whitely against his dark skin. "May I sit down?"

"Yes, of course!" Kit waved absently at the leather-covered couch in the corner. "We'll be comfortable there." As soon as they were settled, she raised her eyebrows at him. "Now, J.B., why did Thack send you here?" Again she spoke before he could answer. "And please call me Kit."

"Okay, Kit." J.B. tilted his bottle to her in salute. "It seems Thack's concerned about this man you're doing business with."

"Man?" Kit frowned. "What man?"

"Flint Falcon."

Kit nearly choked on the wine she'd sipped. "Mr. Falcon! But why would Thack be concerned about him? Thack doesn't even know the man."

"But Thack does know *of* him," J.B. returned softly.

Kit didn't at all care for the sound of J.B.'s statement. "Exactly what does Thack know?" Her eyes narrowed. "And how did he garner whatever it is he knows?"

J.B. favored her with a sardonic look. "You did know Thack's an ex-lawman?" At her brief nod, he continued, "Thack made a few calls. He didn't particularly like what he was told."

Impatience tightened Kit's soft mouth. "All right, Mr. Mysterious. You've got my undivided attention. What *did* Thack find out about Mr. Falcon?"

"He's an ex-con," J.B. said flatly. "He served two years of a twenty year sentence for rape." Ignoring Kit's sharp gasp, he went on in a hard tone, "He was paroled eight months ago for exemplary behavior."

Eight

Damn!"

Kit slammed the apartment door, loudly punctuating her frustrated curse. She had bitten back the expletive numerous times over the previous hour. It felt good to finally release it aloud.

From the moment J.B. had informed her of Flint Falcon's record, Kit could see her hopes for selling the casino within the near future fading like a dust mote on the horizon. She wasn't even positive it was legal for a parolee to own and operate a gambling casino.

It wasn't that Kit doubted that another buyer would turn up, but she'd invested all her aspirations on Falcon and a quick, uncomplicated sale. Now Kit felt as though she'd been moved right back to square one.

For a little while, Kit had been furious at Thack for his interference. But common sense had finally prevailed and she'd accepted J.B.'s calm assurance that the truth about Falcon would have surfaced before long anyway.

Dropping onto a living-room chair, Kit stared morosely at the carpet beneath her feet. To put the frosting on her deflated cake, not only did she no longer have the prospects of a speedy sale, she'd now acquired the unwanted and unnecessary services of a bodyguard as well.

Kit had not given in without a fight, but her brother's gentle concern had vanquished her objections. A dry smile curved her lips as she recalled their phone conversation.

"But, Thack," she had argued heatedly, "I don't need J.B. to look after me! I have been perfectly safe here for months. Besides which, Falcon isn't even here. He had to return to New Mexico two days ago."

"Likely to check in with his parole officer," Thack retorted smoothly. "But, I have this sneaky feeling that he'll be back. And, when he returns, I want J.B. there with you. I wanted to come to Nevada myself, but Barbara hasn't been feeling too well."

Kit frowned with concern. "What's wrong with her, Thack?"

"Nothing serious," Thack replied immediately. "Barb thinks it was something she ate." His tone firmed. "Don't worry, honey. If the symptoms continue, I'll herd her to a doctor—kicking and screaming, if necessary."

The picture Thack verbally painted was clear to Kit. Barbara had adamantly refused to seek medical attention. *And she had appeared so soft and amenable too!* The thought brought a smile to Kit's lips. Thack's next words wiped it away.

"So, J.B. stays until this deal with Falcon is either settled or falls through."

"Thackery! I tell you it's not necessary!" Kit nearly shouted in the hope of breaking through his obstinance.

"Is McKittrick in Tahoe?" Thack countered coolly.

For an instant Kit was tempted to lie to him, then, realizing J.B. could swiftly confirm or deny her assertion, she told him the truth. "No. But he's as close as the ranch if I should need him."

"And exactly how close is the ranch?" Thack purred, setting the fine hairs on her nape tingling.

"Well..."

"I can find that out as well, honey," he inserted when she hesitated.

"North of Reno," she muttered.

"Yeah," Thack snorted. "J.B. will stay in Tahoe for a spell."

"But, Thack—"

"I just found my sister," Thack said, cutting off her protest. "I don't want to see her hurt. Indulge me, honey. I swear, you can trust J.B. with your life."

Kit believed Thack. In the short amount of time she'd known J.B., Kit had come to the conclusion that he was as tough as old boots, and as dependable. There was also no way she could refuse her brother's plea. Kit conceded defeat with a rueful laugh.

"This is emotional blackmail, you know," she muttered indignantly.

"Sure, honey, I know." Thack's tone softened. "But I have just cause for using it."

"And that is?" Kit taunted.

"I love you."

The big stinker! Kit thought, smiling despite her disappointment and frustration. In fact, Kit didn't for an instant think he was a stinker. In truth, she was crazy about the tall brother she had come to know mere weeks ago.

And now, because she *was* crazy about Thack, she was the disgruntled possessor of one mean-looking watchdog in the form of one Josh Barnet—J.B. to his friends.

Now all I have to do is figure out what to do with him!

As it turned out, Kit soon discovered she didn't have to do anything with J.B. Before the end of the following day, J.B. had slipped unobtrusively into the routine of Kit's life. And, before the end of the first week, it was hard for Kit to remember a time when J.B. hadn't been around.

Still, throughout that first day, Kit had asked herself the same question repeatedly: should she call Logan and apprise him of the situation?

The temptation was strong, if only to hear his voice. One fear kept her from dialing the phone every time she lifted the receiver. After the distance and coolness that had grown between them before they parted, Kit was afraid Logan would simply shrug and tell her to have *fun.*

Logan had always been the first one at her side when she needed help, and even at the times she was positive she *didn't* need it. But that was before he'd made love to her. Before he'd discovered her pose of sophistication was exactly that—a pose. And before he'd realized that making love to her could very likely be a threat to his freedom.

Kit didn't call Logan. Logan didn't call Kit. Behind the facade of her usual natural zest for life, Kit was miserable. She had no way of knowing that Logan was suffering the same misery.

What is she doing? How is she feeling? Who is she with? Logan had grown accustomed to the same questions jabbing at his mind with the tenacity of a boxer with a wicked left. After two weeks of the mental beating, he felt as pounded as the boxer's sparring partner.

Once again seeking solace in the hills, Logan let the big roan beneath him pick his way over the slick ground. A heavy frost during the night had painted the foothills with a slippery white veneer. Though the days remained unusually mild for late fall, winter was definitely encroaching. Thanksgiving was only a few weeks away. Before too long the roan's legs would sink deeply into the mantle of white that would blanket the mountains.

Thanksgiving, and then Christmas. Logan had spent the last twenty-three Christmases with Kit and her family. Would he spend this Christmas with her? Did he really want to?

His expression grim, Logan contemplated the approaching holidays. It would be different. Everything had changed. One night, one moment of lost control, had irrevocably altered the relationship between them. He was no longer Logan, the big brother, the protector, the comforter. She was no longer Kit, the madcap teen, the defiant twenty-year-old, the innocent young woman. She was now Kathryn, the woman, free to choose whomever she pleased. And it was beginning to look like she definitely wasn't going to be choosing Logan, the thief of her virginity.

Logan's sharply expelled breath clouded the brisk air. The two week separation hadn't diminished his feelings for Kit. If anything, he was more deeply in love with her than before. *How long could he play this passive role?* he mused, turning the roan toward home with a flick of the reins. Although Logan wasn't quite ready to admit it to himself, at the edge of his consciousness was a growing certainty.

Only that morning Leslie had imparted the information that Kit would be leaving for Las Vegas the following week. Leslie had also told him of her decision to join Kit there. Logan had speculated on Leslie's disclosures throughout the day. Now, as the sun trekked toward the mountains in the west, Logan acknowledged the decision he'd made early that morning. He would accompany his cousin to Vegas. He might even suggest to Kit that they sit down together and have a serious discussion. Beyond that, Logan refused to allow himself to speculate.

Kathryn. Her name curled around his mind like a wisp of smoke, and coiled around his insides like a creeping vine. Eyes wide open, Logan could see her, feel her, taste her. Like the cloud made by his breath, her image formed, her eyes deepened to blue-black with passion, her pale cheeks flushed with excitement, her lips wet and parted in anticipation.

A low groan hurting his throat, Logan closed his eyes to banish the vision. Instead of dissolving, the image grew sharper, more real. As if she were there before him, Logan could see the delicate curve of her throat, the enticing curve of her full breasts, the luring indentation of her waist, the exciting length of her silky dancer's legs and the inviting apex of her thighs that held the promise of ecstatic oblivion.

The roan danced skittishly as Logan shifted abruptly in the saddle. Desire rushed wildly through his veins, to convene in a painful knot in his loins.

"Damn you, Kit!" Logan's harsh cry echoed around the hills and through his head. "What are you doing? How are you feeling? Who are you with?"

Kit went to Las Vegas with J.B. in tow. She really didn't mind; she'd grown used to having him around. Though taciturn by nature, J.B. possessed a dry sense of humor and a swift acerbic wit. In soft asides, he'd make short, succinct character analyses of the people he came in contact with. He was always right on target.

"Mike's a tiger posing as a dandy," J.B. had observed early in the first week he was at the casino. Of course, he was correct. Before the end of that week, he and Mike were in perfect accord.

Also before the end of that first week, Kit knew exactly where she stood with J.B. To her combined delight and chagrin Kit realized she'd gained another champion. Thack reaffirmed her belief.

"The guy's crazy about you, honey," Thack had drawled the last time Kit spoke to him. "In a brotherly sort of way, if you know what I mean."

Kit knew too well what Thack meant. There were times she felt surrounded by brothers, protectors. There were even times when she wondered if there was a quirk in her femininity, since the only men who seemed physically attracted to her were the ham actor-beach bum sort. All the real, pulse-stopping men she knew just wanted to *protect* her. Hell, even Mike treated her like a young sister!

Except for Logan—and that one night. Regardless of what she was doing, who she was with, Logan was always on her mind. She had spent the majority of the two weeks since she left the ranch alternately damning *him* for letting her go and *herself* for letting him off the hook without a fight.

She loved him more than ever. Being with him, belonging to him, if only for that one moment, had solidified her love. Her nights were torture. During the daylight hours, Kit could keep the memory of their brief time together at bay. But when she was alone in the night, the memory defeated her, aroused her, tormented her. It was when she lay alone in her bed that Kit sometimes believed she could actually see Logan as he had been that night, breathtaking in his male beauty, exciting in his arousal. And it was then that Kit despaired of ever getting what her body had so quickly learned to crave—having her needs assuaged by Logan again.

Though Kit was surprised when, near the end of the second week, the call came for her to be on the set on the coming Monday, she was relieved at the prospect of having something new to do that might prove a diversion. When she called Leslie to invite the older woman to join her in Las Vegas, Kit had to bite back a request to speak to Logan. She had given herself joyfully to him—mind, heart and body. The next

move was up to him. And Kit was beginning to be terrified that Logan was never going to make that move.

Las Vegas was as Las Vegas always was, garish,
gaudy, and exciting. Here were casinos that diminished hers by comparison. Here were all the illus-
trious names in the entertainment field. Here were all
the hot-eyed gamblers and pleasure-seekers, from the
mind-boggling rich to the down-to-the-last-dollar
poor. And here was the small, independent company
on location for a low-budget, tightly scheduled film.

The film was to be a character study—most of the
characters seedy. The lead part was a gambler whose
luck had run out. The female protagonist was a law
enforcement officer who was on the take. The small,
two-scene role that Kit was to play was that of the
gambler's bubble-brained girlfriend, who he stran-
gles early on in the film. Kit had accepted the low-
paying role simply because she'd always wanted to do
a death scene.

"Ready on the set."

The set was on the stage of the cabaret in one of the
smaller casino hotels. The scene was the finale of the
show and the confrontation between the showgirl
bubble-brain and the gambler.

"Camera's rolling."

Along with nine other leggy young women, Kit
high-kicked her way into the stage wings. Her lips
twisted nastily as she spotted the gambler, standing
off to the side. Grabbing a towel, she stormed up to
him.

"You gotta nerve comin' for me tonight!" Kit lifted
her lip in a sneer.

"Wadda you talkin' about, doll?" the gambler whined, his eyes wide in surprise. "We have a date to party tonight—remember?"

"Yeah, I remember," Kit retorted. "I've got a good memory. I remember real good who I saw you with last night."

The gambler went dead still. His eyes shifted. "What did you see?" He grabbed her arm, his fingers digging into the soft flesh. "Who did you see?"

"That oh-so-proper lady cop," Kit said, yanking her arm free, then rubbing the bruised skin. "And I use the term 'lady' loosely. That broad's on the make." Kit arched one heavily penciled brow. "Is she also on the take, I wonder?"

"You shut your mouth," hissed the gambler. "Or I'll shut it for you."

Kit spun away from him, her eyes flashing. "Don't threaten me, you jerk! I've got friends in this town."

"Cut! That's a wrap."

The director's words were like balm to a heat rash for Kit. Exhaling sharply, she grinned at the weary-looking actor. "How many times did we do that scene?"

"I forgot an hour ago." The actor grinned back. "Ask the kid over there with the call-board."

Wiping her face with the towel, Kit turned away. "I'll pass, thank you. I'm not sure I really want to know anyway."

Making her way around cameras, cables, lights and assorted people, Kit found the backstage door that opened into the cabaret. The room was empty but for a few invited spectators. Her guests were seated in one of the curved, richly padded booths near the center of the room. Kit's steps faltered as she approached the group. When she had left the booth before going onto the set, her spirits had been soaring. Kit had expected Leslie to arrive since she had invited her, not only to Vegas, but onto the set. She had not expected Logan.

The sight of him—big, broad, endearingly familiar—made the breath catch in Kit's throat and her knees tremble. Logan had never visited any of the film sets she'd worked on, had never shown the slightest interest in her work. What had he thought while watching her? she wondered, suddenly nervous.

Sitting at the end of the booth facing her, J.B. was the first to notice Kit as she came up to them. A tender smile softened his usually austere features.

"Well done, honey," he complimented her. J.B. had adopted Thack's casual endearment for Kit near the end of his first week in Tahoe.

A flush of pleasure suffused Kit's cheeks. "Thank you." She returned his warm smile before sliding her glance to Logan, waiting, hoping he'd remark on her performance as well. Logan's expression gave her a sinking sensation in the pit of her stomach.

His face had a closed, forbidding look. His eyes were the dull, flat green of an unpolished stone. His lips were little more than a slashed line above his rigid jaw. There was a tautness about him that radiated inner fury.

Baffled by his coldness, Kit stared at him blankly. *Why was he so angry? Had Logan and Leslie argued?* Searching for an answer, Kit glanced at the other woman. Leslie was grinning at her like a child delighted by an unexpected surprise.

"Oh, Kit, I'm so pleased you invited me here to-day!" Leslie exclaimed, sliding off the end of the seat to embrace her. "You were great. I had no idea you possessed so much acting talent." Releasing her, Leslie stood back, a frown lining her smooth brow. "Why in the world do you continue to audition only for bit parts? And why, for heaven's sake, haven't you come to New York to try out for the theater?"

Praise indeed! Kit laughed in astonishment. An actress herself, Leslie had had numerous successes on the Broadway stage. If Leslie said Kit was good, chances were she was right. Leslie's comment about New York didn't surprise Kit; she was well aware of Leslie's disdain for Hollywood.

"I—I never even considered trying out for the stage," Kit finally found her voice to reply. "I enjoy working on films, but I've never had a burning desire to be a star."

"Shame on you," Leslie scolded with a chiding smile. "You're wasting a God-given talent."

"On a two-bit film." There was a scathing bite in Logan's tone. A bite Kit had never heard from him before. "With a two-bit company."

Startled, Kit sliced her gaze back to him. If anything, he appeared even more angry and his eyes looked positively lethal. Kit marshaled her arguments to defend her acceptance of the role, and the company, but before she could speak, Leslie was questioning him.

"You think she's good also, don't you, Logan?"

"Yes, she's good," Logan retorted. "But, like everything else, she's merely playing at it."

Stunned, hurt beyond belief, Kit stared at him mutely while J.B. and Leslie rushed to her defense.

"Logan! What are you saying?" Leslie demanded in a shocked tone.

"That's a little heavy-handed, isn't, McKittrick?" J.B.'s voice was warningly soft.

Holding J.B.'s narrow-eyed stare, Logan slid from the booth. "Sometimes the truth is." A challenging light flared in his eyes. "I know our Kit," he went on cynically, "I know her one whole helluva lot better than you or your boss. Oh, yeah, Kit's a damn good player—at life as well as at acting." A bitter smile curled the corner of his lip as he gazed momentarily at Kit, then, with a dismissive shake of his head, he walked away.

"Logan!" Leslie's cry went unheard by the big man and Kit.

"Well now, hang me for a fool." J.B.'s murmur also failed to reach Kit, as did the speculative smile that curved his lips.

Devastated, blinking rapidly against a hot surge of tears, Kit watched Logan's retreat, and bit her lip to keep from calling after him.

I've lost him! I've lost Logan. The refrain beat in her head. And she realized she'd lost not only the man, but her most steadfast champion. Kit was suddenly certain she knew why she had lost him. By giving in to the need to have him make love to her, she had convinced Logan she was *playing*—at love as well as at life.

The clicking sound of a lighter and the pungent scent of cigarette smoke filtered through the hypnotic bemusement gripping Kit. Dazed, she glanced from the now empty entrance of the cabaret to the woman standing beside her.

"I don't know what's the matter with Logan," Leslie murmured distractedly, drawing deeply on the long, slender cigarette. "He's so moody and restless."

"He get like this often?" J.B. inquired interestedly.

"No, very rarely, in fact." Leslie lifted her shoulders in a helpless gesture. "Logan is usually even tempered and caring of other's feelings." She glanced at Kit. "Isn't he?"

"Yes," Kit sighed.

J.B. contemplated the two women solemnly. "How long has he been like this?"

"For weeks." Leslie frowned. "He was moody and rather short-tempered that morning you left to return to Tahoe—remember Kit?"

I'll probably never, ever forget. Kit kept the thought to herself, and nodded briefly in answer.

"I'm beginning to worry about the possibility of him having a health problem." After one final draw, Leslie crushed the cigarette in the ashtray on the table.

Logan's problem is more emotional than physical. Staring into space, Kit kept that opinion to herself also. "I don't think there's a health problem," she said softly.

"Well, then maybe it's me." Leslie bit her lip. "Maybe he's tired of me running to him and crying on his shoulder every time *I* have a problem."

The lost-child sound of Leslie's voice snapped Kit out of her self-absorbtion. "Oh, Leslie, that's ridiculous, and you know it!'' she exclaimed. ''Logan loves you. He always has.''

''He's always loved you, too,'' Leslie reminded her. ''Yet he was actually cruel to you just now. Maybe we've both worn out our welcome and his patience.''

Not you—me. ''Maybe,'' Kit hedged, dropping her gaze. A tiny frown drew a line on her brow as she noted the wrapper covering her costume; she had completely forgotten about changing! ''Will you look at me!'' Kit forced a laugh. ''I've got to remove this makeup and get out of this costume!'' She glanced from Leslie to J.B. ''Will you two wait for me?'' Kit couldn't prevent the forlorn note that crept into her tone; she just didn't want to be alone right now.

''Of course we'll wait.'' Leslie smiled in understanding.

''But not here,'' J.B. said flatly. ''I want a beer.'' He grinned at Kit. ''You know we've been here for hours.'' Cupping Leslie's elbow, he said teasingly, ''C'm'on, Red, I'll buy you a drink.'' He winked at Kit. ''We'll be in the lounge off the casino floor, honey.'' As Kit spun away, he called, ''I'll have a glass of wine waiting for you, so don't dawdle.''

''You're a bossy, cantankerous pain in the—'' Kit began chidingly.

''I do my best, honey,'' J.B. shot over his shoulder, determinedly steering Leslie from the room.

Kit's smile lasted for all of ten seconds as she hurried from the cabaret to her dressing room. *Logan.* His name revolved in her mind as she stood under a stinging shower spray. *Logan.* An image of him tormented her as she dressed in tailored slacks, a raw silk shirt and slip-on, narrow-heeled shoes. *What was she going to do about Logan?*

What the hell was he doing here?

Logan grimaced at the foamy head bubbling at the top of the beer glass on the table in front of him. It was not yet dinnertime, but the lounge was three-quarters full of very obviously thirsty people.

Logan wasn't even thirsty, but he raised the glass and downed half the the amber contents in three deep swallows. A sour taste, unrelated to the beer, rose in his throat.

Damn, he'd hurt her. The wounded look that had shadowed Kit's eyes refused to be banished from Logan's mind. He had lashed out at her because of jealousy and fear. Self-disgust left the sting of bile on his tongue.

Sighing, Logan settled back in the padded, curved-armed chair. The live entertainment had taken a fifteen-minute break. The thump of drums and the twang of guitars had given way to the muted roar of animated conversation. Logan was the sole occupant in the lounge without a table companion. The table he'd deliberately chosen was positioned in a corner, allowing him a clear view of the dimly lit room, while affording him some privacy; Logan desired solitude, not company.

Jealousy and fear. God, how he hated it. Logan sipped absently at the cold beer. He wasn't exactly wild about the constant sexual ache clawing at his body, either. But, to a degree, he'd lived with the ache for over eight years and, though it had been bad at times, he'd at least had the option of finding physical release with another woman. Logan no longer had that option. No other woman would do for him.

Having tasted the excitement of Kit, there was simply no other flavor sweet enough to satisfy Logan's appetite.

Because he had no choice, Logan knew he could live with the physical ache of need, but he wasn't as certain of his ability to deal with the more destructive emotions of jealousy and fear.

Restless, uncomfortable with his thoughts, Logan moved in the chair, then went dead still as his roving gaze caught sight of the perpetrator of his plight. Eyes narrowed, he watched J.B. seat Leslie at a nearby table.

Honey. Logan silently sneered the endearment, and damned the man who had used it. He had first heard the man use it when Kit had introduced Logan and Leslie to J.B. on their arrival at the cabaret early that afternoon. J.B. had called her that again less than an hour ago.

While they'd waited for the film company to set up the scene Kit was in, J.B. had not given any explanation for his presence in Nevada. The man had just said that he was a friend of Thack's. Logan couldn't help but wonder exactly what had occurred between Kit and J.B. during the previous two weeks. The seed of suspicion had been planted with J.B.'s initial use of the term "honey." It grew into an ugly sprout with his enthusiastic praise of her performance and subsequent use of the endearment.

Had Kit exercised her newly found freedom with the cool, watchful J.B.? That question was the cause of Logan's fear.

Never before had Logan experienced the sickening urge to pound another human into the ground, not even when he and Zack had broken into that hotel room to wrest Kit from the actor. Logan had longed to break Drake's face, but not to literally pound him into the ground.

Yet now, observing J.B.'s easy smile and Leslie's animated response to the laconic Texan, Logan was consumed with a feeling that bordered perilously close to killing hatred.

If he's touched her, I'll kill him. Logan closed his eyes as the vow filled his mind. *Damn it! Kit is mine!*

Nine

That is one very rattled man.

Listening to his thoughts, J.B. smiled encouragingly at Leslie, who was still raving about Kit's performance in the short scene they'd observed. While he heard every word the beautiful redhead said to him, a part of J.B.'s mind gave cool consideration to his speculative thoughts.

"You can tell that much from watching her for such a brief period of time?"

"Certainly." Leslie's elegant eyebrows peaked, displaying a hint of arrogance. "I've been in the business for a long time. I can recognize natural talent."

J.B. conceded the point with a single nod. Though his gaze remained fixed on Leslie's animated face, with his peripheral vision he could see Logan McKittrick sitting alone at his out-of-the-way table. A ghost of a smile curled the corners of J.B.'s thin lips.

The big rancher looked about ready to explode.

J.B. fought a strong desire to laugh out loud. After two solid weeks of practically nothing to do, things were definitely looking brighter. Perhaps now he'd see a little action, he mused. And not at the gaming tables, either.

The action started a few minutes later with the arrival of Kit. Enjoying himself more than he had in months, J.B. had the sensation that he could actually feel the muscles in Logan's imposing form tighten as he assisted Kit into the chair close to his.

I'll give him sixty seconds. J.B. sliced a quick glance at his watch as he reseated himself. A moment later he concealed a grin by glancing down at his wrist. His guess had been short by thirty seconds. An intimidating scowl on his rugged face, Logan was rising from his chair. Pretending ignorance of the rancher's approach, J.B. deliberately leaned to Kit to murmur an innocent compliment into her ear.

The burning sensation in Logan's stomach burst into an inferno as he watched J.B.'s lips brush Kit's ear. A haze of red fury blanketed his common sense at the tinkling sound of Kit's delighted laughter.

One-armed or not, I swear I'll plant him!

Logan's lethal thought didn't show on his frozen features as he came to a stop at Kit's table—nor did the sharp pain that cut into his chest as her expression altered from pleasure to dismay.

I've killed whatever feelings Kit had for me. The realization intensified Logan's pain. *My Kit. My Kit. Why did you let me love you? Did you know that by giving me a taste of your sweetness, you'd be condemning me to a life of agony?*

"I want to apologize for my boorish behavior," Logan said quietly. *I want to shake you for letting me have you, then turning away from me,* he said silently.

The words were stilted and his tone was strained. Gazing up at him, Kit had the uncanny sensation of the bottom falling out of her heart. "You're entitled to your opinion, Logan." Kit sadly acknowledged that her own words were as stilted, her tone every bit as strained as his.

The tension grew as the silence lengthened. Leslie finally broke the uneasy atmosphere. "Why don't you sit down, Logan? Have a drink with us?"

"I've had a drink." *Abrupt, much too abrupt.* Logan cursed himself for his lack of control. He worked up a faint excuse for a smile. "It's almost dinnertime, and I've barely seen the inside of my room since we checked into the hotel this morning." Logan and Leslie had not taken rooms in the hotel they were now in. "I want to run downtown and have a shower."

Leslie drank the remainder of her Manhattan. "I think I'll go with you. I want to shower and change, too." An impish smile brightened her eyes. "If I don't do it before I venture into the casinos, I'll still be in these clothes at dawn tomorrow morning." Sliding her chair back, she stood beside Logan.

"You were planning to gamble all night?" J.B. asked in a tone of assumed shock.

Leslie tossed her mane of fiery hair in a gesture of carelessness. "Doesn't everybody?" she replied.

J.B. sent a swift, assessing glance from Leslie to Kit to Logan, before returning his attention to Leslie. "Sounds like fun to me," he drawled, draping his arm with apparent casualness over the back of Kit's chair. "Why don't we make it a foursome for dinner, gambling and breakfast?" He gently but noticeably pressed his fingers into Kit's shoulder as he subtly emphasized the word *we*.

Logan's features seemed to lock into a frigid mask, but before he could form printable words of refusal, Leslie and Kit spoke simultaneously.

"I don't know..." Kit began, eyeing Logan warily.

"Oh, yes, please, let's!" Leslie pleaded enthusiastically. "It's been ages since I've had a night out for no other reason but my own enjoyment."

Recalling Leslie's devastated appearance at the ranch two weeks ago, Kit didn't have the heart to refuse her. Neither did Logan. Which was exactly what J.B. had counted on. Smiling mysteriously, he checked the time.

"Okay, let's synchronize our watches." He raised his dark eyebrows. "How does an hour and a half sound?"

"Perfect," Leslie decided. "Oh! And let's have dinner at some wildly expensive restaurant."

"It's your night," J.B. murmured indulgently. "You choose."

Leslie immediately named a French restaurant with a reputation for exorbitant prices. Then they left the lounge to go their separate ways, Leslie and Logan to the hotel downtown, and Kit and J.B. to where they were staying on the strip.

The minute she was safely alone in her hotel room, Kit dropped onto the bed to stare blankly at the ceiling. She didn't want to have a night out in Logan's company. She didn't want to get within miles of Logan. Logan didn't like her anymore.

Hot tears rushed to sting her eyes and then trickled warmly down her pale cheeks. Logan didn't like her anymore. Disjointed and out of order, memories flashed through her mind, memories of the times Logan had dropped whatever he was doing to hurry to her side when she needed him, for whatever reason.

There had been the instances when Kit had felt that she really didn't need or want his assistance. But there were also the instances when she'd relied on his presence. Her mother's funeral was the most clear in her mind.

Though Zack had been there for her, Kit had felt it necessary to make a show of strength in front of her brother. It had been in Logan's arms that Kit had sought comfort, on Logan's chest where she had sobbed out the misery of her loss.

And now Logan didn't like her anymore. And all because she had given in to her hunger for him, the need to know him in the ultimate union of a lover.

Giving way to despair, Kit sobbed out her unhappiness. When the wrenching shudders subsided to tremors, she lay spent, her mind and purpose clear. Never again would she turn to Logan for protection, or comfort, or understanding. She had infringed on his time and freedom long enough. Having assured him of her maturity, Kit knew she now had to prove that assurance.

Rolling to the edge of the bed, Kit glanced at her watch as she sat up. She had less than half an hour in which to shower, repair the ravages her tears had inflicted on her eyes and do something with her mussed hair.

She'd had her hour of mourning what had been and what would never be again. And, though Kit knew she'd survive, she was determined to survive in style. Ignoring the sensation of emptiness inside, she leaped from the bed and strode into the bathroom to prepare for the first test to her new maturity.

Kit was fastening the scarlet and gold-toned cloisonné clip to the loose knot she'd arranged her hair into when J.B. rapped gently on the door. Drawing a breath, she ran a final, critical gaze over her image in the mirror.

Her ash-blond hair gleamed silvery in the glow from the dresser lamp, the upswept style elegant, yet casual with the fine tendrils that curled enticingly against her nape. Her makeup was minimal, underplayed to allow the natural glow of healthy youth to shine through, yet alluring with the sweep of her lashes darkened and her eyelids shadowed. Her silk dress was simply cut, yet dashing with its plunging neckline and rich red shot with gold color. Her hose was sheer to the point of nonexistance. Her sandals consisted of a few supple leather gold straps and high, narrow heels. Blind to her own attractiveness Kit didn't see the breathtaking picture she presented. J.B. did.

"Be still my heart." J.B.'s drawl contained a hint of awe as Kit swung out of the room. "Lady, you are a walking threat to every man's libido," he complimented her, offering his arm to escort her to the bank of elevators.

Flushed with pleasure, Kit sent him a teasing, sidelong glance. "For a cowboy, you look right smart yourself," she murmured approvingly, sweeping his lean body with an appreciative glance of surprise.

Used to seeing J.B. in jeans, scuffed boots, a wellworn shirt and somewhat battered denim jacket, Kit was stunned by the change in him. His navy-blue, three-piece suit enhanced the muscular slimness of his body and deepened the sapphire shade of his eyes. His crisp, white shirt contrasted effectively with his dark skin and hair. His black, soft leather shoes were buffed to mirror shininess. A black leather glove encased his left hand.

"I'd say we make a damned fine looking couple," J.B. observed as they waited for the elevator. "Wouldn't you?"

"A damned fine looking couple," Kit concurred laughingly.

"Just might do the trick."

Kit missed his remark as the elevator doors swished open at that moment. Smiling dryly, a sheen of expectation sparking brightness in his eyes, J.B. followed Kit into the lift.

"Damn!" Logan smoothed the hairbrush through the shock of auburn waves one last time, then threw it onto the dresser top in disgust. His eyes narrowed as he stared morosely into the mirror at his untamable mane. Giving his hair up as a lost cause, he took stock of the rest of his body. His suit was one shade darker than his hair and fit neatly to his broad-shouldered body. His shirt was tan, with the mere suggestion of pink. His tie was a solid color of darker tan, and was already making Logan feel as though he were strangling.

With a twist of his lips, and a slight jerk of his head, Logan dismissed the image in the mirror. He didn't want to go out to dinner, gambling and breakfast. Most especially, he didn't want to go out with Kit and J.B.

Had she slept with him? Was she sleeping with him?

Logan could not turn away from the questions as easily as he turned away from the mirror. The same questions had bedeviled him ever since he'd first heard J.B. call Kit "honey" in that caressing tone of voice.

Pushing back the cuff of his shirt, Logan scowled at the face of his watch. It was time to traipse down the hall to Leslie's room. But, damn it, he didn't want to go out!

Logan crossed to the phone in three long strides, determined to beg off from the night of fun and frolic. *Some fun,* he thought sourly, grasping the receiver. His idea of fun was not watching another man make love with his eyes to the woman *he* was in love with.

"Damn J.B.'s eyes," Logan snarled, lifting the receiver.

While waiting for the switchboard operator to connect him to Leslie's room, Logan had second thoughts. A vision sprang into his mind of how excited Leslie had looked when they'd made the date. It was the first time he'd seen her looking so eager and alive since she'd arrived unannounced at the ranch over two weeks ago. With a sigh, Logan resigned himself to a very long, probably agitating evening. He simply asked Leslie if she was ready when she answered the phone.

Logan's apprehensions about the evening proved correct, starting from the moment the two couples met outside the restaurant, and ending in the coffee shop where they watched the sun rise as they ate breakfast.

J.B. murmured asides to Kit throughout dinner, easing her tension, making her smile. For, with Logan's attitude of cool remoteness, Kit was positive she couldn't have eaten a morsel of the delicious food she was served or chatter away to Leslie as if nothing at all was out of the ordinary.

It wasn't quite as difficult for Kit once they started making the rounds of the casinos. By mutual consent, they all went their separate ways, in pursuit of whatever game interested them, agreeing to meet at a preselected place every hour or so.

Logan was so cold and silent at the breakfast table, Kit was grateful for the sheer exhaustion that numbed her senses.

But Leslie apparently had had a wonderful evening, for she insisted the four of them meet again that evening for a reprise. Kit might have been able to hold out against the pleading redhead if J.B. hadn't supported the suggestion.

"Why not play for a while?" J.B. seconded Leslie's motion, smiling tenderly at Kit. "When your work's complete on the film it will be back to the grind at the Silver Lining."

Watching Kit, neither Leslie nor Logan noticed the smile J.B. quickly hid when Kit grimaced at the mention of her casino. Logan did, however, notice her grimace and his expression hardened even more.

But, in the end, they all gave into Leslie's plea for continued self-indulgence. And so they slept for the majority of the daylight hours, and gambled and gamboled through the night.

By the time they met for breakfast the third morning, Kit was an emotional wreck. Logan had withdrawn to the point of an automaton, responding tersely, inflectionlessly, to everything and everyone.

Again, had it not been for J.B.'s murmurs of encouragement and caring concern, Kit knew she'd have run screaming all the way back to Tahoe. After a lifetime of dependence on Logan's moral and emotional support, Kit also knew she couldn't take much more of his cold disinterest. As desperately as she loved him, wanted to be with him, Kit admitted that if she didn't get away from the stranger he'd become, she would be running the risk of disgracing herself by begging him to love her again—if only as a sister and valued friend.

So it was with the conflicting emotions of relief and regret that Kit received Logan's flatly issued refusal when, as they finished breakfast, Leslie went into her now familiar cajoling routine for one more night of play.

"Count me out." Logan's tone was heavy with absolute finality. "I've got a ranch to run." Not quite true since he employed an extremely knowledgeable foreman. "I'm leaving as soon as I can get my gear together."

"You're flying out this morning?" Leslie asked the question on Kit's lips.

Logan nodded in answer. "I'm going home."

Home. Yes, Kit thought, that's where she wanted to be, needed to be. And she would go home the minute she completed the work she'd been contracted for on the film. But not to Tahoe. She would have to stop over in Tahoe, of course, to either sell the casino, if Falcon were still interested, or promote Mike to full manager. On the spot, Kit decided to go home, all the way home, to California and Zack, the brother who genuinely loved her.

In self-defense, and for the sake of self-preservation, Kit would not allow herself to remember how she had always thought of Logan's ranch as her true *home*.

The sun sparked glaring flashes of light off the small window next to Logan as the plane banked to approach the landing strip at the airport in Reno. The brilliant shards of sunlight pierced Logan's tightly closed eyelids. Weariness dragging at his spirit as well as his body, Logan stirred and slowly sat up straight.

He didn't as much as glance through the sparkling pane; Logan knew what the terrain looked like as well as he knew every inch of his own property. And he knew from now on he'd be seeing a lot more of it.

It was over. After twenty-five years of single-minded devotion to protecting, guiding, loving Kathryn Aimsley, it was over. Logan had the sickening sensation of not only having lost a part of himself, but of having had that part brutally torn from his body.

He would forget her. Logan wondered how many times he had assured himself of his ability to banish the memory of Kit.

How? Logan had lost count of the times the small inner voice asked the unanswerable.

Didn't they say that time heals all wounds? Logan challenged the inner voice.

You don't have that much time left, the voice chided softly, *not even if you live to be one hundred and twelve years old.*

She doesn't want me. Logan continued to argue with himself as he walked to where he'd parked his car. *She's found a new protector. A new friend. A new— lover.*

And, of course, that was why he was now here— dead on his feet from too many nights of *playing* and too little sleep. Logan knew that had he not left, he would have given in to the urge to bloody his knuckles on the face of her new protector, new friend, new lover.

Logan was not by nature a violent man. The growing desire to maim another human being filled him with disgust. By removing himself from proximity to Kit and J.B., he had exercised his only rational option.

But that didn't make it hurt any less.

The call came for Kit to be on the set two days after Logan departed Las Vegas. Shuddering with relief, she anxiously looked forward to finishing her work with the scene that was scheduled to be shot the following morning.

Kit died magnificently.

Only four takes were required to complete the scene and then she was free. Over a salad lunch Kit barely touched, she gently informed Leslie of her plans to return to Tahoe later that afternoon.

"And I'm going back to Manhattan," Leslie said, lifting her head regally. "I've decided it's time to face the real world—and the bastard I married." Reaching out impulsively, she clasped hands with her companions. "And I have you two to thank for helping me reach that decision."

"But we didn't do anything!" Kit exclaimed laughingly.

"That's where you're wrong," Leslie corrected. "You proved the value of life to me by example."

"But—" Kit began to protest.

Leslie cut her off with a sharp shake of her head. "You—" she inclined her head toward Kit "—by example, showed me that life is worth living, even if you feel emotionally crippled." Leslie turned her attention to J.B. who was silently observing the exchange. "And you, by example, shamed me by confirming the joy possible in life, even if one is physically crippled." Leslie's eyes were bright with tears by the time she finished speaking. So were Kit's. J.B.'s smile was tender with compassion.

"Come see me," Kit whispered to Leslie as they parted company.

"If you're ever in Texas, I'll be there," J.B. murmured, embracing Leslie's trembling body.

"I will," Leslie responded to Kit.

"I'll remember," she promised J.B.

And then they went their own ways—Leslie back to the East Coast, Kit and J.B. back to Lake Tahoe.

The first thing Kit did after arriving at the Tahoe apartment was flip on her telephone answering machine to play back the recorded messages. She removed her jacket as she listened to Mike's familiar voice.

"Zack called. He said to tell you the date has been set. You're to get in touch with him as soon as you get back."

Kit smiled as she waited through the brief pause on the machine. Her brother was getting married. Kit was at once both happy and sad. Logan. Mike's voice came from the machine again as Kit blinked away a surge of tears.

"Mr. Falcon called today." Mike gave the time and date. The time was ten-sixteen, the call had come that very morning. "He said to tell you he is ready to talk seriously. And, if Logan proves difficult, he'll look elsewhere. He sounded adamant, Kit. Here's the number you're to call to reach him." After Mike relayed the number the machine clicked off.

If Logan proves difficult. The phrase revolved in Kit's mind while she unpacked her suitcase, showered and pulled on a nightgown and knee-length robe. Logan had done nothing *but* prove difficult!

Entering the living room from her bedroom, Kit eyed the telephone, her lips thinning, her chin jutting at a determined angle. She was going back to California either way. But she would prefer going back free of the encumbrance of the casino.

Striding to the phone, Kit grasped the receiver. She would tackle Logan one last time.

"Hello." The endearingly familiar sound of Logan's voice weakened Kit's knees, and resolve. "Hello?" he repeated impatiently. "Who is this?"

Kit strengthened her flagging courage with anger.

"It's Kathryn, Logan," Kit used her proper name haughtily, deliberately. "I'm back at the apartment in Tahoe. Mr. Falcon called while I was away."

"I'm impressed." Logan's tone of weary boredom infuriated Kit and drove the thought of caution from her mind.

"I don't give a *damn* whether you're impressed or not!" she retorted scathingly. "I want out. Out of this business, and out of this state." She paused to draw breath, then continued grittily, "You told me you'd talk to Falcon. Are you going to stick to your agreement?"

Silence hummed on the wire connecting them, then Logan inquired tauntingly, "What will you do if I say no?"

Convinced that was exactly what he was going to say, Kit literally saw red. "I told you I'm getting out. And now I'll tell you what I'll do. I'll see my lawyer to instruct him to sign the entire casino over to you." She hesitated briefly, then went on bitterly, "With an addendum detailing exactly what you can do with it." Angry beyond rational thought, Kit slammed the receiver onto the cradle.

Having spent the last few days working himself to a standstill to avoid having to think at all, Logan was also beyond rational thought. Cursing violently, he threw his receiver onto the cradle and stormed from the ranch house.

He'd had it! Spewing stones and dirt in his wake, Logan manhandled his car along the ranch road to the highway. Conversely, instead of cooling off during the long drive to Lake Tahoe, he got hotter with each passing mile.

By the time he parked the car at Kit's apartment, Logan was barely thinking at all, never mind rational. Grim-lipped, he nodded in response to the security guard's greeting. "Evenin' Mr. McKittrick."

The flaming rage consuming Logan's mind spread to heat his entire body. Logan shrugged out of his sheepskin jacket as he rode the elevator to Kit's floor. About to explode, he strode along the hall to her door, then jabbed at the door bell. Logan had not formulated exactly what he was going to say to Kit, he'd been too furious. When Kit opened the door, the vulnerable-looking sight of her gave him pause. Had she not raised her chin defiantly and glared at him, his anger might have dissolved.

"What the hell do you mean—" as he spoke he backed her into the room "—you'll tell me exactly what I can do with the casino?"

Ignoring the frisson of fear the slamming door sent skipping down her spine, Kit came to an abrupt stop. "I mean exactly what you think I mean," she snapped, meeting his blazing green-eyed stare with challenge. "I told you I want out. I want to get away from here. I don't care if I never see Nevada again."

"Or me, either, I suppose?" Logan's tone was warningly soft.

Kit ignored the warning. "Or you, either," she agreed, sweeping his imposing form with a dismissive glance.

Logan's eyes narrowed. Had Kit not been so very angry herself, she might have noted how dangerous Logan was at that moment. But Kit was angry, disillusioned and hurting. And, like most animals in pain, human or otherwise, she lashed out blindly.

"I want no part of you, Logan McKittrick!"

Logan stiffened, then closed in on her menacingly. "You've found a new—" his lip curled "—playmate?"

Kit's eyes flashed blue fire. Rising up on her toes, she leaned forward, close to his face. "That is none of your damned business, McKittrick." She enunciated each word with hard emphasis. "But I'll tell you this. *If* I have found a playmate, you can bet your a—saddle, he treats me like an intelligent, mature woman!"

Logan's eyes narrowed to mere slits. His muscled chest heaved with anger. His long fingers clenched and opened spasmodically. But before he could speak without turning the air blue with expletives, Kit thrust her face even closer to his, close enough to catch the tangy smell of his spicy after-shave.

"And I'll tell you something else, *mister*," Kit gritted softly, no longer even aware of what she was saying, but flinging words designed to injure him and bolster her own sagging ego. "*He* won't be handling me with kid gloves, like a fragile piece of porcelain, either."

Logan's fingers curled into his palm, tightening until the knuckles turned white. "What are you saying?" he demanded in a tone hoarse with strain.

What *was* she saying? Kit didn't allow herself an instant to ponder. Smiling suggestively, she taunted, "I'm saying he'll take me as I wish to be taken, fast and hard, because that's the way both of us want it."

Logan flinched as if he'd been physically struck and then, acting on reflex, he struck back. His hand shot up to grasp her hair, arching her slender neck as he tugged her head back.

Bending over her, he stared into her widening eyes. "Well, if that's what you want," he said in a whispered snarl, "I'll be more than happy to accommodate you."

As he growled the last word, his mouth crashed down onto hers.

Ten

Shocked, for a few moments Kit fought his kiss, his crushing embrace. Then, never thinking that she'd confirm his statement by her action, she went pliant in his arms.

This was Logan—Logan's mouth was demanding a response from hers, Logan's tongue was demanding entrance. With a sobbing moan, Kit curled her arms around his taut neck and returned his kiss with her own hungry demand and arched her empty body into the hard readiness of his.

Kit's abandoned response fired Logan's blood, canceled his thoughts, broke his control. Groaning in answer to her throaty moan, he gripped her to him fiercely then released her to tear at her robe and nightgown. He felt the vibrations of her gasp at the sound of material being rent.

"I have no intentions of treating you like a fragile piece of anything," he muttered into the moist warmth of her mouth.

Through the passion clouding her mind, Kit heard the sound of her filmy nightgown being ripped from her body, felt the cool air caress her heated flesh. But even as a distant voice insisted she protest his rough treatment, the erotic rhythm of Logan's greedy tongue stole the initiative from her and silenced the puny voice.

The room spun crazily as Kit was swept up into his arms, and had barely settled again before she was literally flung onto her bed. The breath rushed out of her with a whoosh as she landed. Rattled, disoriented, Kit blinked, then stared as she caught sight of Logan.

Illuminated by the glow of moonlight streaming through the wide bedroom windows, Logan looked wildly dangerous and grimly determined as he pulled the clothes from his muscular body. A heady tingle of combined excitement and fear doubled her heartbeat. The pulse in her throat throbbing erratically, Kit wet her parched lips as Logan tugged the socks from his feet, then stepped out of his jeans and narrow navy briefs.

"Logan?" Kit's reedy voice held a question and a hint of a plea. Logan misunderstood the latter.

"Don't worry, *Kathryn*," he assured her in a darkly sexy tone. "I won't disappoint you." One broad hand captured her breast as he stretched his length on top of her and nudged her legs apart with his hard thighs. "You will have it as you wish."

Sliding his other hand beneath her, Logan lifted her body to meet the thrust that sheathed him within her. A gasp of sheer, exquisite pleasure broke from her parted lips. Instantaneously, her body moved to match his cadence.

"Fast and hard." Logan's voice was rough, his breathing ragged as he drove himself relentlessly. "Exactly as you want!"

An explosive mixture of flaming anger and rampant passion impelled the increasing strength of Logan's thrusting body. One unformed thought remained, driving him ever deeper into the moist sweetness of her. The vague thought centered on one key word.

Mine. I must make her *mine.* I will make her *mine.*

The key unlocked the door to paradise.

"Mine!" Logan shouted the word as his life force burst forth.

"Mine," he gasped as he felt Kit's shuddering contractions tighten her body around him.

In trembling reaction, Kit lay exhausted, listening to Logan's breathing slowly return to normal. Satiation of her body induced lucidity of thought. What had Logan meant with his outcry? Had he rejoiced because *she* was his, satisfaction was his—or victory was his?

Kit's mind went cold as her body cooled. *Victory.* Kit's eyes frosted. Logan had attacked to prove a point. She had deliberately enraged him. He had retaliated most effectively. He was the victor. She was the vanquished.

Because she loved, she was punished. The emptiness inside, so briefly filled, yawned like a chasm in her body, in her mind. Suddenly Kit hated Logan almost as much as she loved him. Determined to reveal nothing of her weakness, she pushed impatiently against his shoulders with trembling hands.

"If you're quite through with your ravishment," she said in a disinterested tone, "I'd like to go to sleep now."

Logan's relaxed body tightened, then he pushed himself away from her. Kit saw the rigid cast of his strong jawline—and missed the alarm flaring in his eyes. The moment he left the bed, she turned her back to him.

"I thought you wanted to discuss Falcon." Logan's voice was completely devoid of expression.

"I don't care," Kit mumbled into the pillow. "Either way, I'm going home, back to California—to stay." Though Kit managed to keep her tone even, she could not control the tears that dropped onto the pillow.

"What about this place?" The faint sound of rustling clothes could be heard as he asked the question.

"I'm going to sell it." Adamancy roughened her voice. "Now, will you please just get out?" Kit knew that if he didn't go very quickly, she'd disgrace herself by breaking down in front of him.

"All right, I'll go." His voice was harsh, dismissive, his tread heavy as he walked to the bedroom doorway. "And you can have the damned casino. Sell it to Falcon or give it away." His tone was flat. "I couldn't care less."

I know. Kit closed her lips on the anguished response. Inhaling deeply, calmingly, she turned to look at him, her eyes remote, her face composed. "Lock the door on your way out, please."

"With pleasure," Logan returned tauntingly. "With as much pleasure as I'll lock you out of my life." And then he was gone, leaving devastation in his wake.

The backlash hit Logan like a blow as he was driving out of Tahoe. The tremors rippling through his big body increased to shudders, which swiftly accelerated to a severe case of the shakes. Pulling the car to the shoulder of the road, Logan shut off the engine and rested his head on the steering wheel.

"Kit. Oh, God! Kit."

Logan's anguished moan seemed to fill the car's interior and beat against his conscience. His beautiful baby. His endearingly gawky teenager. His maddeningly exciting young woman. Kit had been all those people to him, all those and more. Her life had forever been intertwined, woven through the pattern of his. Now he had severed the last thread, broken the lifeline, altered the pattern.

"Lock the door on your way out."

Kit's final words revolved in Logan's mind, growing louder and louder, hammering at him like the mocking scream of a demented person.

Out. Out of her home. Out of her thoughts. Out of her life. Forever—out.

Logan swallowed repeatedly against the sickening surge of self-disgust that rose like fire to burn in his chest.

And he had accomplished this feat of stupidity all by himself.

"Damned fool."

The muttered condemnation fell like a shimmering teardrop into the late night silence.

Kit wasn't shuddering, or shaking, or weeping. As still as death, she lay rigid on the bed, staring sightlessly at the nothingness that was now her life.

You are young, an inner voice soothed. *There will be another man for you to love.*

Kit dismissed the inner voice with a faint smile resembling a sneer. She didn't feel young, she felt very old, and incredibly tired. Dry-eyed, drained of emotion, she acknowledged that even if she *made* love with some future man, she would not *love* that man. Kit's love belonged to the man who had locked her out of his life—*with pleasure.*

Logan had been a part of her life from her beginning and, willing or not, he would own her heart until her end.

Resolution, if not renewed energy, came with the first pale light of dawn. She had made the decision while still in Las Vegas. She would now act on that decision. She was going home.

"When you set your mind on something, you're a regular dynamo." J.B. made the coolly voiced observation as he stashed his battered valise in the crowded trunk of Kit's car.

"I want to get back to California." Kit's tone was flat, as devoid of life as it had been throughout the previous week, ever since the morning after Logan had granted her permission to sell the casino and ordered her to stay out of his life.

"Obviously." J.B.'s tone was dry. After securing the trunk lid, he circled the car to slide into the bucket seat on the passenger side. Kit settled behind the wheel. "And McKittrick?" he murmured, watching her narrowly.

"What about him?" Kit's flat tone didn't falter.

J.B. hid a compassionate smile. "Just curious," he admitted with a shrug. "I would have thought he'd want to sit in on the meeting with Falcon yesterday."

"He's a busy man." Kit was careful not to mention Logan by name. "And it really wasn't necessary for him to be there."

They were referring to the meeting held the day before, the meeting that had set the wheels in motion that would eventually free Kit of the responsibility of the casino.

As promised, Flint Falcon had returned to Lake Tahoe. Understanding came for Kit during the meeting when it was revealed that Mr. Falcon had been completely exonerated of the crime he had been convicted of. If Falcon harbored any bitterness for having been robbed of two years of his life for an act of violence he didn't commit, it didn't show. Kit felt positive she would not have been as calm and cool under the same circumstances.

"Logan's lawyers can handle the details for him when I come back for the closing on the sale." Kit made the statement as she set the car in motion and drove away from the condominium complex. Although she didn't want to, Kit knew she would have to return to Nevada. She made a promise to herself that it would be the last time she would return. "My lawyer will take care of all the details of selling the apartment after the sale of the casino is complete." A hint of hard finality shaded her tone.

"I'm surprised you didn't keep the apartment for a vacation home." J.B. watched Kit's competent movements as she eased the car into the flow of highway traffic away from Lake Tahoe.

"If I want a vacation," Kit retorted, "I'll go to Hawaii."

J.B. released the grin he could no longer suppress, and silently applauded her grit. Although he was certain that *something* had happened between Kit and Logan after her return from Vegas, something that had hurt her badly, he was just as certain she was not about to discuss it. Kit hid her pain well. While cynically amused by the way two seemingly intelligent people could screw up each others lives, J.B. still admired her tenacity. Kit had pushed herself unceasingly during the previous week untying all the knots that bound her to Nevada.

And now they were on their way to California and a wedding.

J.B.'s grin smoothed into a soft smile. "You could always vacation in Texas," he suggested, easing his body into a more comfortable position. "You're always welcome, you know."

"I'll keep it in mind." Kit returned his smile. She was going to miss J.B. Now that the threat surrounding Flint Falcon had been eliminated, she had no need for a bodyguard. "I suppose you'll be glad to get back after the wedding, won't you?" When Kit had called Zack to tell him she was returning to California for good, he had asked her to bring J.B. with her.

"I've talked to Thack," Zack had said. "He and Barbara will be arriving about the same time you plan to get here. If J.B. comes along with you, he can return to Texas with them. Besides, I've heard so much about him that I'd like to meet him."

"It's home."

Kit frowned. Into her thoughts, she'd missed J.B.'s quiet response to her question. "I'm sorry. What did you say?"

J.B. chuckled. "I said, Texas is home."

Home. Kit had the hollow sensation that the word would haunt her for the rest of her life.

The wedding was beautiful.

Even in a state of surprised shock, Kit was aware of the beauty surrounding her. The ceremony was held in the spacious courtyard in her brother's unique multi-level complex along the Big Sur. Warm fall sunshine bathed the gleaming copper statue of a kneeling woman before which the bride and groom solemnly repeated their vows.

Aubrey, Kit's brand new sister-in-law, was radiant in ivory silk. Standing side by side, Kit's brothers, Zack and Thack, looked like handsome bookends cast in gold. Seated between Kit and J.B., Barbara glowed with an inner radiance, sparked by love for her husband and the secret hope that their love had created a new life inside her.

Kit would have felt serene had it not been for the tall, formidable man standing on the fringes of the crowded courtyard.

Kit had been certain Logan would not show up for the wedding. She'd been wrong. He'd arrived minutes before the ceremony, looking cool and withdrawn and heart-shatteringly attractive.

As soon as the ritual of kissing and congratulating the newlyweds was over, Kit avoided Logan by adroitly moving from one group of guests to the other, laughing and conversing with old friends, introducing herself to unknowns. She had no idea how much time had elapsed when, as she moved from one cluster of guests to another, J.B. halted her progress by lightly grasping her by the arm.

"What is it?" Kit frowned as he led her across the yard to the gate that gave access to Zack's private bluff overlooking the Pacific.

"I want to talk to you." J.B. inclined his head to indicate the path bordering the bluff. "You can stop running now," he murmured, pausing to gaze out over the ocean. "He's gone."

"Who's gone?" Kit was unsuccessful in achieving a tone of mild inquiry.

J.B. smiled knowingly. "McKittrick—and you know it. He left right after the ceremony."

Kit tried a brief shrug; she was unsuccessful at that, too. "Zack told me Logan was very busy at the ranch. I suppose he had to get back." Actually, she didn't believe it for an instant. Neither did J.B.

"Bull," he said distinctly.

"What do you mean?"

J.B. shook his head pityingly. "You know damn well what I mean. Logan didn't *have* to get back. He's retreating."

Yes, Kit agreed silently. Whenever Logan had had enough of her he retreated to his ranch. And this time he'd had enough to last him a lifetime. Kit stared bleakly at the gently undulating sea below.

"That man's bleeding to death inside."

"What?" Kit's head jerked up and around. Her eyes were wide with fear. "Is Logan ill?"

"Oh, yeah, he's got an illness. It's called love."

Kit shook her head, denying J.B.'s diagnosis. "You're wrong."

"I'm right." J.B. raised his hand, silencing her when she started to speak. "I earned my living by observing people, reading them. And Logan's symptoms are easy to read. That man is so crazy with love for you, it's eating him alive inside. At this point, I'd bet Logan doesn't know whether to scream, swear, or throw stones at the moon." His lips twisted wryly. "Reactions all caused by frustration, anger, and soul-destroying unrequited love. The man loves you, honey."

"Yes, I know he does." Kit kept her tone light, even though her world was very dark. "Logan has always loved me." She stepped around him nimbly, and smiled overbrightly. "He loves me in exactly the same way Zack and Thack do." Smile in place, Kit moved away from J.B., back toward the courtyard where there was noise enough to block out her own dismal thoughts, one of which demanded, *but why did he make love to me?*

Watching Kit literally run away from him, J.B. shook his head sadly. Then his eyes narrowed as an idea sprang to his mind. A slow smile curved his lips.

"Well," he murmured, his smile widening into a grin. "If you can't snare the filly, go after the stallion." Laughing softly, J.B. followed Kit back to the reception.

Four days later, Kit sighed wearily as she shut the door of the apartment in Tahoe. Although she had never envisioned the sale of the casino going through so quickly, Kit was not annoyed at being called back to Nevada so soon. Since Zack and Aubrey were honeymooning in Mexico, and Thack, Barbara and J.B. had departed for Texas two days ago, Kit had swiftly grown tired of her own company and thoughts—most of which centered on Logan.

Logan. Shoulders dropping, Kit walked to her bedroom, coming to an abrupt stop as her glance collided with the bed.

Oddly, after her absence, Kit felt Logan's presence in her bedroom more strongly than she had mere minutes after he'd stormed out of it. It was having Logan shut her out of his life that was crushing the spirit out of her.

After showering quickly, she curled up on the bed. She was tired; she needed rest. She had a meeting at nine in the morning, a meeting that would conclude the sale of the casino. After the meeting any reason for her to remain in Nevada would be removed. Curling into a ball of misery, Kit shut her eyes tightly, trying to banish the sound of J.B.'s voice echoing in her mind.

"The man loves you, honey."

Kit was neither rested nor refreshed the next morning when she entered her office for the last time. She had forty-five minutes until the nine o'clock meeting, more than enough time to clean out her desk.

Some twenty minutes later, Kit was dumping the contents of desk drawers into the large shopping bag she'd brought with her when the intercom buzzed. Distractedly shoving the drawer into place with one hand, she depressed the Speak button with the other.

"Yes. What is it?"

"Mr. Falcon to see you, Ms. Aimsley," Kit's secretary said brightly.

Falcon? Kit frowned and bit her lip in consternation. "Ah . . . send him in, please," she responded, silently praying that he hadn't changed his mind about buying the casino at the last minute.

The difference in appearance in the man who strode into Kit's office was a shock to her entire system. For all his quiet voice and politeness during their previous meetings, Kit had always been wary of the man. There was a cold, remote intenseness about him that was more than off-putting—it was downright scary.

This morning, Flint Falcon's sharp features were somewhat relaxed, if not actually easy. His black eyes, usually drilling in their directness, appeared lighter, if not actually soft. A meager smile curved his usually tight, forbidding thin lips. In total, Falcon gave the impression of a marginally satisfied man.

Kit was definitely not satisfied. Afraid of what he might say, yet needing to know, she plunged into speech as he quietly closed the office door. "There's a problem, Mr. Falcon?"

"Not at all," the dark-skinned man returned promptly, revealing glistening white teeth in the closest thing to a real smile Kit had ever seen from him. "Just the opposite, in fact." His movements were so light, so graceful, he appeared to glide across the room to her desk. "I stopped by merely to look at the place." A deprecating smile twitched his lips. "Your floor manager told me you were here." Falcon lifted his shoulders in a shrug. "I thought perhaps we could go to the meeting together."

Logan was already exceeding the speed limit, yet he pressed his booted foot more firmly against the gas pedal.

If he harms her I'll kill him, he thought savagely, slicing a glance to the mile marker along the side of the road. Ten more miles to go. Damn! Logan pressed his foot into the pedal.

The tension coiling inside Logan had increased with each passing mile throughout the long drive to Tahoe from his ranch, tension spawned by a lethal combination of fear and anger. Logan's potentially explosive emotional state had been caused by an early morning telephone call from Texas.

"Kit has a nine o'clock meeting with Falcon today." J.B.'s tone had been deceptively casual.

"I know that." Logan had to fight to keep his own tone steady while wondering why the one-armed, ex-cop had returned to Texas without Kit. J.B.'s next question sent a finger of dread skipping icily down Logan's spine.

"Did you also know that Falcon is an ex-con?"

"What?" His mind suddenly alert to danger, Logan missed the purrlike quality to J.B.'s tone.

"Um-hmm. He served two years for rape." There was a slight pause. "The woman was white."

The woman was white? What did that mean? Logan shook his head. "What are you getting at, Barnet?" he demanded harshly.

"Why nothing." J.B.'s voice was pure innocence. "It's just that there's always such an outcry when a white women is attacked by a half-breed."

Logan had never, by nature or inclination, been prejudicial concerning his fellow man. He had always judged a man by *what* he was, not what race or color he happened to be. But love, mixed with a dash of anger and fear, does strange things to a man's reasoning process—as do the words *attack* and *rape*.

And now, nearing his destination, Logan's reasoning process had been completely taken over by one terrifying thought: Kit was alone, unprotected and in the company of a man who had been condemned by a jury of his peers!

His thick auburn hair tousled by his raking fingers, Logan burst into Kit's office just as Flint Falcon was curling his hand around her elbow to escort her from the room.

Logan didn't notice Kit's calm expression, or Falcon's solicitous attitude. All he really saw was the man's hand against Kit's slender arm. The fear and fury in him boiled over, erupting from his tight throat in snarled curses.

"Falcon! If you as much as bruise her, you're dead!"

Descending like an avenging angel, Logan stormed across the room. Grasping the other man by the upper arm, Logan nearly lifted Falcon off his feet as he jerked him away from Kit.

"Logan!" Kit's shocked voice came out in a shriek. "Are you out of your mind?"

Logan was beyond hearing. His green eyes glittering with intent, he flung Falcon against the wall, then slowly closed in for the kill. Before he'd taken two steps he found himself facing death in the form of a wickedly gleaming, narrow-bladed knife that suddenly appeared in Falcon's slim-fingered hand.

"Careful, cowboy." Falcon's voice was as soft as a caress. "I don't know what this is all about, but I'm not waiting to ask questions, either." His tone dropped even lower. "I'll section you like a chicken."

"And I'll break your neck before you can make the second slice," Logan promised, his tone every bit as hair-raising. His move toward Falcon broke the shock immobilizing Kit.

"For God's sake, Logan!" Without conscious direction, she flung herself across the room and between the two men. "What do you think you're doing?" she demanded shrilly.

"Protecting you." Logan's gaze remained steady on Falcon. "As I always have."

"Protecting me!" Kit repeated in a baffled screech. "Protecting me from what?"

"This man is a rapist, Kit," Logan growled. "Now get out of the way." Moving cautiously, he raised his hand to push her out of harm's way.

"He's been exonerated!" Kit shouted. Suddenly furious and thoroughly fed up, she knocked his hand out of the way.

"Exonerated?" Logan murmured, eyeing the grim-faced Falcon warily.

"Yes. He has proved his innocence." Kit's throat was tight from exasperation. "Mr. Falcon is not a rapist," she said grittily. "And you are not Gala-had."

Suddenly unsure, Logan flinched at the anger sparking her eyes to blue ice. "Kit..."

"We have an appointment, Miss Aimsley," Flint Falcon said smoothly over Logan's hesitant voice. "If you and Mr. McKittrick could continue this, ah, con-versation later?" Dry amusement etched his thin lips.

"Yes! Of course." Kit glared at Logan, then turned her back on him and walked from the office beside Falcon.

It was truly over. Feeling drained, Kit rested her head on the wall of the elevator car as it ascended to her floor. The meeting was over; the sale of the casino was complete. Kit's embarrassed apologies to Flint Falcon for the scene in her office had been profusely made. Logan was gone—very likely back once again to his hideaway ranch. Kit was exhausted.

The elevator doors slid apart with a soft swish. Pushing herself erect, Kit walked into the hall, her steps faltering at the sight that met her tired gaze.

Logan was standing sentinel outside her apartment door, his gaze fixed on her progress. Lines of weariness scored his rugged face, his green eyes were opaque with apprehension.

Kit didn't notice. As she resumed walking toward him, her mind replayed each and every time Logan had come to her *rescue*—regardless of whether she needed rescuing or not. As she remembered each successive scene, Kit's steps grew firmer. Renewed anger sent a charge of energy surging through her. Not bothering to look directly at him, or speak to him, Kit unlocked the door and stalked into the apartment. She spun to face him challengingly when she heard the door close softly.

"I'm sorry—" That was as far as she allowed him to go.

"Not as sorry as you're going to be!" Kit exclaimed, fully incensed. "I am sick and tired of being treated like a wayward child, Logan McKittrick! I mean—"

"I know," Logan interrupted. "But, damn it, Kit, when J.B. called I just—"

"J.B.!" Kit cut him off, astounded. "J.B. called you?"

"Yes!" Now Logan was shouting. "He told me about Falcon's record. And how he got it." He raked his hand through his already wildly ruffled mane. "God, Kit, he scared the hell out of me!"

"But J.B. knew Mr. Falcon had..." Kit's voice trailed away as understanding filtered through her anger. "That son-of-a-gun." She laughed chokingly. "J.B. was playing cupid!"

"Cupid?" Logan frowned, then his eyes narrowed contemplatively. "Are you telling me J.B. was trying to prod me into some form of action?"

Kit stiffened, and raked her mind for an answer that would not betray her feelings. But Kit was tired. Tired of it all—most especially the dodging, the hedging, the sheer stupidity of it all. Raising her chin, she looked him squarely in the eyes.

"Yes, I believe J.B. was deliberately prodding you." A faint smile tilted her lips. "He had a go at me the day of Zack's wedding."

"Had a 'go' at you?" Suddenly Logan looked every bit as dangerous as he had in her office earlier. "You'd better explain—and it better be good." He began closing in on her.

Kit took a step back, then stopped, her heart beginning to beat crazily from the burst of excitement inside. Logan was *jealous*! The realization robbed her of breath for an instant. That whole, miserable time in Las Vegas—Logan McKittrick had been furious with jealousy over J.B.! Silently vowing to hug J.B. at the first opportunity, Kit tossed her head regally.

"After you retreated to the ranch," she finally answered, "J.B. advised me to follow you." Head high, breath suspended, Kit waited.

Logan frowned. "Why did he suggest that?" Logan asked in a tone Kit prayed carried a note of hope.

"J.B. said you were bleeding to death inside," Kit said distinctly. "And that you were crazy with love for me."

Logan stiffened a moment, then exhaled sharply. "So?"

Kit's patience ran out. "So! J.B. also knows I'm desperately in love with you, you lunkhead!" Planting her hands on her hips, Kit glared at him, very *un*lovingly.

"Are you, Kit?" Logan murmured in a suspiciously rough voice.

The half hopeful, half fearful expression he was not quick enough to hide drained all the starch from Kit's spine and filled her eyes with warm tears. "I have been for over eight years, Logan."

"Not as a sister?" he asked rawly.

"No." Kit shook her head sharply.

"As a woman?" he persisted.

"Yes." Kit nodded once, definitely.

"Thank God." Reaching out, Logan hauled her into his arms. "Oh, my Kit, J.B. was right. I am crazy with love for you."

There was a lot more to be said, many explanations to be given. But there was time for that later. There was a whole lifetime later. Here, now, there were the two of them—in harmony at last.

It was unimportant whose mouth sought whose; that the contact was made was enough. Both thrilled to the sweet taste of love shared. Clothes were a hindrance to be swept aside; touch was paramount. The bed was a haven for two. When Kit arched to him eagerly, Logan held her still.

"Patience, darling," he murmured against her trembling lips. "I want to live out all my fantasies about you. I want to make love to you slowly this first time."

"But we've made love before!" Kit exclaimed, frowning when he shook his head.

"We had sex before." His lips curved excitingly. "Good sex, but sex just the same. Now we're going to make love."

Logan's hands were gentle, reverent as he explored Kit's body, learning the sensitive areas that drew husky gasps of pleasure from her. His teeth nipped lovingly, his tongue bathed sensually as he coaxed her nipples into gem-hard arousal. His fingers probed delicately as he tested the heat of her desire.

Eager to know all of him, Kit returned the loving attention. Her palms tingled as they glided over his smooth skin and the tautened muscles beneath. Her lips burned with anticipation as his flat male nipples tightened at her kiss. Her mind spun in a whirl when he groaned as her fingers enclosed the hard readiness of his manhood.

And through all of it, the low murmurs of love exchanged fired the senses of both.

"Your skin's so silky."

"You're so very strong."

"Your legs are gorgeous."

"Your chest is magnificent."

"I love the taste of you."

"Your flavor's more tangy than champagne."

"I love you more than my own life."

"I adore you."

The growing restlessness of mutual touches increased the tension demanding release in their bodies.

His mouth hungry on hers, Logan eased his body into the cradle of Kit's thighs, moaning as her soft hands enveloped him to guide his passage.

"Heaven," he whispered as his body joined with hers.

"Home," Kit sighed, arching to accept all of him.

It wasn't till near dawn when Kit and Logan ventured from the bedroom—though they had both awakened with a mutual hunger much earlier. Stretching like a well-fed cat, Kit eyed her husband of less than two days, a satisfied smile curving her lips: she and Logan had spent the majority of those two days in the bedroom of the ranch line cabin in the mountains. The cabin had been Kit's choice of the perfect honeymoon site.

"You're wearing a smug expression, woman." Logan's lips brushed her ear as his arm curled around her waist, drawing her to the hard warmth of his body. His breath caressed her skin as he laughed softly. "A smug expression and very little else." His hand stroked the silky material of the robe Kit had pulled over her nakedness.

"Look who's talking," Kit chided, turning into his arms. "That toweling robe you've got on leaves little to the imagination. And you're looking rather self-satisfied yourself."

Logan nuzzled her neck. "Hours and hours of exquisite lovemaking will do it to me every time," he assured her in a serious tone.

Laughing, Kit twirled out of his arms. "I love you madly, McKittrick, and I'm loving our honeymoon, but I'm starving!"

"Nag." Catching her hand, Logan started for the tiny kitchen. "Let's see what we can rustle up in a hurry." He was halfway across the living room when Kit tugged on his hand.

"Logan, wait! I want to see if it's still snowing."

His smile indulgent, Logan moved with her to the door, then onto the roofed porch.

"Oh, it's stopped." Kit sighed in disappointment. "And I was so hoping we'd be snowed in here till spring."

A chuckle rumbling in his chest, Logan drew her into his arms, cradling her close to his warm body. "It hasn't fully cleared," he murmured soothingly, gazing up at the overcast dark sky. "Maybe we'll get lucky."

At that moment a large bank of clouds moved, revealing the full white moon. Kit gasped in wonder as the snow-covered ground and heavily snow-laden pine branches were bathed in a silvery glow. Logan didn't notice the scene before them. His gaze was caught by the silvery sheen of moonlight dancing in his wife's pale hair.

"Beautiful," Kit murmured, referring to the winter world.

"Beautiful," Logan agreed, referring to the woman he loved more than his own life. "But cold." Tightening his embrace, he turned them as one and led her back to the warmth of the cabin. "And I'm hungry."

"And here I was just thinking you were sexy." Kit glanced up at him mischievously. A slow smile curved Logan's lips.

"That comes after breakfast."

Silhouette Desire

COMING NEXT MONTH

WHAT THIS PASSION MEANS—Ann Major
Her father had taught Rex everything he knew: Kate had given him her innocence. He'd left them both. Now she needed Rex to help retrieve a sunken galleon . . . but revenge came first.

THE SOUND OF GOODBYE—B J James
When Victoria Mallory fled her childhood home, she left behind a fairytale world, and the only man she'd ever loved. Eight years later Ben was the owner of the Mallory Mansion—and the tables had turned.

A FRAGILE BEAUTY—Lucy Gordon
When Maurizio Varelli informed her that she would marry him and not his younger brother, Vicki's dreams were shattered. Maurizio was a man accustomed to having his way, and he intended to possess her—body and soul.

THE SKY'S THE LIMIT—Syrie A. Astrahan
Grant knew that Kelli was just the woman to complete the ad campaign for a Lake Tahoe casino—not to mention his life. He soon found himself setting out on his own campaign: to win her heart.

GAME, SET, MATCH—Ariel Berk
Carson had had his share of the lime-light during his pro-tennis days. But Phoebe was determined to tempt him from his reclusive life in rural Vermont, and prove to him that love could be a winning score.

MADE IN HEAVEN—Annette Broadrick
Despite her protests, Denice was forced into a loveless union by her manipulative father. Could she and Brant learn to trust one another enough to make the marriage real?

AVAILABLE NOW:

RAGE OF PASSION
Diana Palmer

MADAM'S ROOM
Jennifer Greene

THE MAN AT IVY BRIDGE
Suzanne Forster

PERFECT TIMING
Anne Cavaliere

YESTERDAY'S LOVE
Sherryl Woods

NEVADA SILVER
Joan Hohl

**Available
January 1987**

NEVADA
SILVER

The third book in the exciting
Desire Trilogy by Joan Hohl.

The Sharp brothers are back, along with
sister Kit...and Logan McKittrick.

Kit's loved Logan all her life and, with a little
help from the silver glow of a Nevada night,
she must convince the stubborn rancher that
she's a woman who needs a man's love—not
the protection of another brother.

Don't miss *Nevada Silver*—Kit and
Logan's story and the conclusion
of Joan Hohl's acclaimed
Desire Trilogy.

A NOTE FROM THE AUTHOR

While working on the Desire Trilogy, several subcharacters knocked on my occupied mind, demanding stories of their own. Those characters were: Peter Vanzant, Josh (J.B.) Barnet and Flint Falcon. Annoyed by their persistence, I told them to pick a number and get in line. They did.

The first one to queue up was Peter Vanzant. Not especially pleased with Peter's rather cavalier treatment of Barbara in *Texas Gold*, I smiled diabolically and gave him *Lady Ice*, a Silhouette Desire that will be published later this spring. Hopefully, the Lady will teach Peter a few lessons about life in general—and love in particular. We'll see.

Joan Hohl